MW01657129

THE SNAKE'S SONG

Also by Mary E. Lowd

Otters In Space

Otters In Space 2: Jupiter, Deadly

Otters In Space 3: Octopus Ascending

In a Dog's World

The Necromouser and Other Magical Cats

The Snake's Song

A Labyrinth of Souls Novel

by

Mary E. Lowd

ShadowSpinners Press

Cover art by Josephe Vandel.
Book design by Matthew Lowes.

ShadowSpinners Press
shadowspinnerspress.com

Typeset in
Minion Pro by Robert Slimbach
and IM FELL Double Pica by Igino Marini.
The Fell Types are digitally reproduced
by Igino Marini, www.iginomarini.com.

Learn more about
the Labyrinth of Souls game at
matthewlowes.com/games.

For my mother, husband, daughter, and son. With special thanks to Nina Kiriki Hoffman—without her writing dates, I would never have written this novel.

Editor's Preface

Dungeon Solitaire: Labyrinth of Souls is a fantasy game for tarot cards, written by Matthew Lowes and Illustrated by Josephe Vandel. In the game you defeat monsters, disarm traps, open doors, and explore mazes as you delve the depths of a dangerous dungeon. Along the way you collect treasure and magic items, gain skills, and gather companions.

Now ShadowSpinners Press is publishing this and other stand-alone novels inspired by the game. Each *Labyrinth of Souls* novel features a journey into a unique vision of the underworld.

The Labyrinth of Souls is more than an ancient ruin filled with monsters, trapped treasure, and the lost tombs of bygone kings. It is a manifestation of a mythic underworld, existing at a crossroads between people and cultures, between time and space, between the physical world and the deepest reaches of the psyche. It is a dark mirror held up to human experience, in which you may find your dreams … or your doom. Entrances to this realm can appear in any time period, in any location. There are innumerable reasons why a person may enter, but it is a place antagonistic to those who do, a place where monsters dwell, with obstacles and illusions to waylay adventurers, and whose very walls can be a force of corruption. It is a haunted place, ever at the edge of sanity.

The Snake's Song

1

THE SNAKE SANG.

The snake sang and mice knew better than to listen.

Mice and rats and songbirds and frogs—none of them listened to snakes. Songbirds and frogs sang their own songs; mice and rats told stories. None of them listened to snakes.

And neither did squirrels.

But one day, a gray squirrel named Witch-Hazel stopped to listen to a soft hissing carried on the wind, a susurrus coming from a tunnel, hidden beneath a bush. With melancholy sighs and mesmerizing murmurs, the hissing voice sang a song of days gone by, days long ago when the earth and sky and underground were bound together with a river that flowed in endless, looping circles; tree branches embraced the heavens, and tree roots held the depths in their woody arms; and all the creatures of Earth could make a pilgrimage into the sky to meet the All-Being who had created every animal.

"What happened?" Witch-Hazel chittered, her voice small and filled with wonder. She had never heard any story or song like this one before. Squirrel stories were about storing nuts for the winter, finding buried treasure that you'd forgotten, and squabbles over who got to live in the best branches. They were small. This song was the size of the entire world.

From the darkness under the leafy boughs of the bush, the whispering song answered: "The world cracked."

Witch-Hazel chittered in alarm, as if the world were cracking now beneath her fuzzy feet. Her bushy tail quivered, and she felt the need to dart up a tree and hide in the highest branch. But she didn't follow her instinct. The story had her hypnotized, and she barely flinched when she saw the twin pools of gold resolve in the dark of the bush.

Snake eyes. Staring at her. Unblinking.

"The world cracked, and we are all shattered fragments, a poor broken reflection of the All-Being who created us."

"Tell me about the All-Being," Witch-Hazel asked breathlessly.

"The All-Being is why birds can fly, fish breathe water, beavers are builders, and bees can turn pollen into honey. Each of them reflects the glory of the All-Being."

Witch-Hazel wondered how she reflected the All-Being's glory. "How about squirrels?" she asked.

The golden pools withdrew, deeper into the leafy darkness of the bush, and the hissing voice drew in a sharp breath. "Squirrels can find lost treasure."

Witch-Hazel was disappointed. She remembered with shame the shining trove of chestnuts she'd buried last autumn. She'd searched for them all winter, digging under every tree root that bumped out of the ground just-so, but none of them had been the right root on the right tree. Her sisters and brothers had shared their troves with her, keeping her fed through the bitter cold months.

Witch-Hazel was not good at finding things.

"I'm a poor reflection of the All-Being then," Witch-Hazel said, grabbing her bushy tail and grooming it for comfort.

"Maybe you're not good at finding things that don't matter," the voice hissed.

Witch-Hazel was doubtful. Those gleaming meaty chestnuts would have made the winter much easier. They had mattered to her. Still she wondered what exactly the hissing voice meant. "What kind of treasure would matter?"

"The Celestial Fragments." After those three words, the voice stopped like a sudden cessation of wind, and the stillness that followed was unsettling.

Witch-Hazel had an eerie sense that she'd heard those words before. She reached deep into her memory, and the phrase recalled a sensation of dry grass, crumpled leaves, and the flavor of mother's milk. She'd heard those words when she was a tiny kitten, she realized, tucked safely inside her mother's nest, still nursing with her littermates. The Celestial Fragments were part of a fairy tale told to kittens.

"You've heard of them?" the snake hissed. Its voice had lost some of its power.

"Yes," Witch-Hazel agreed, backing away from the bush, realizing that she'd been falling under a snake's spell. "The Sun Shard, the Star Sliver, and the Moon Opal." She glanced toward the nearest tree, readying to dart away, but not wanting the snake to suspect she'd escaped its thrall. So she kept talking, "One grants strength, another endless breath, and the third flight—but they're nothing more than a fairy story for kittens."

"Are they?" the snake hissed, withdrawing deeper into the bush, either giving Witch-Hazel space to feel comfortable or preparing to strike. The gold pools of its eyes disappeared into the mottled darkness of the leaves. "Strength, flight, and endless breath are traits of the All-Being; they are also the traits you would need to find the All-Being."

Against her better judgment, Witch-Hazel asked, "Where is the All-Being?"

"High in the sky," the snake answered. "Deep in the blue ocean above us that was left behind when the rivers that once encircled the world dried up."

"Why don't the birds sing of the All-Being then?" Witch-Hazel asked. "Surely, they know everything in the sky."

"They cannot fly high enough," the snake hissed from the darkness. "And even if they could, the birds couldn't breathe up there in the sky-ocean. It would take the strength of a bear, the wings of a bird, and the endless breath of a fish to reach the All-Being." With a final teasing, hissing sigh it said, "The Celestial Fragments are down here. You could find them."

Then the snake was gone.

But the ideas it had left in Witch-Hazel's head were not. They lingered between her tufted ears. They wouldn't go away. They haunted her, possessing the little squirrel with an enchanting image: she would find the Celestial Fragments; she would take on their powerful aspects; she would meet the All-Being and look upon the creator of all creation.

Something deep in her soul was soothed by the image of herself staring the All-Being in the eye. She saw all the aspects of the animals in this world pulled together in one remarkable creature and understood the way that she, herself, fit into the entirety of creation, represented in one being.

Witch-Hazel pictured a creature with one bat wing and one sparrow wing; a green cat eye and a yellow coyote eye; a long rabbit ear and a round mouse ear; a deer antler and an antelope horn; a hoofed foreleg and a webbed paw; a mountain lion's golden haunches and a squirrel's silver tail—because no creature on Earth has a tail more beautiful than a squirrel.

The little squirrel stared at the bush until she could almost make out the shape of the All-Being in its mottled leaves as they swayed in a light evening breeze. The air swept coolly across her own fur, and Witch-Hazel was startled to realize the day was almost over. She'd spent hours under the snake's spell. And she wasn't sure she'd truly recovered from it.

She didn't know if she ever would.

That night, Witch-Hazel slept in her poorly made nest of leaves in the crook of a branch in her favorite oak tree. Her brothers' and sisters' nests were warm and cozy at night; they knew how to weave dried grasses, leaves, and twigs together into the walls of a comfortable home. Somehow, the leaves in Witch-Hazel's nest never behaved so well—the leaves crumbled, twigs broke, and the whole thing flew apart whenever there was the slightest wind. She wasn't very good at being a squirrel.

But she might make a good adventurer.

She wanted to find the Celestial Fragments.

In her nest that night, Witch-Hazel felt the empty space all around her. The air flowed around her branch like the rivers the snake told her had once encircled the under-earth and sky. She wanted to travel those rivers.

The next morning, Witch-Hazel made her decision. Whatever treasures could be found beneath the earth, she intended to find them. But first, she needed to prepare.

So Witch-Hazel dug up the only stash she could find—a clutch of black walnuts that she'd stolen from a brother and hidden in a crocus bed only a week before; then she dug up the crocus bulbs and the bulbs of a few early tulips. They were easy to find, pointed to by their tender green shoots. Witch-Hazel packed the bulbs and walnuts in a knapsack along with a blue winter coat her mother had crocheted and a few leaves from one of her namesake bushes—witch-hazel leaves were a useful medicine. Then she swiped a flask of pear cider from her biggest sister's nest—her sister wouldn't mind—and stuffed that in the knapsack too.

Finally, Witch-Hazel left a note in her own nest for her sisters and brothers, in case they came looking for her: "Gone adventuring. Don't worry. —Witch-Hazel"

They wouldn't come looking. They wouldn't worry. They'd simply be glad she'd stopped mooching off of their winter stores and asking to squeeze into their nests on the coldest nights. Still, just in case, she left the note. It was what her mother would want her to do.

With serious doubts regarding her own sanity, Witch-Hazel slung the knapsack over her back and headed for the snake's bush. In all likelihood, there was nothing beneath the bush but the snake's den. And the snake. Possibly a hungry snake.

Witch-Hazel needed to arm herself.

The little squirrel skittered through the grove of oak and elm trees, making her way toward the sprawling firethorn bush. In the autumn, the emerald bush would burst forth with brilliant red berries. The berries were bitter and always hurt Witch-Hazel's stomach, but they were plentiful. Better than a hungry night. Right now, though, the firethorn bush was covered in sprays of white flowers. And thorns.

Witch-Hazel broke off two long thorns and tucked them into a woven-grass belt she wore. Now she was armed with wooden swords longer and sharper than the snake's fangs. The swords made her feel safe. Although she knew it was sheer craziness to enter a snake's den, she also felt it would be crazy to continue living her quiet life of petty frustrations, hiding nuts and losing them, when there was a chance she could discover the lost Celestial Fragments beneath the Earth.

Witch-Hazel made it to the snake's bush and entered the leafy darkness with both firethorns drawn. Her paws quivered, and her tail twitched nervously. Yet she felt like the Sun Shard, Star Sliver, and Moon Opal were calling to her. She could hear them singing her name, begging for her to find them.

Witch-Hazel squeezed into the small round hole under the bush. She'd never entered a snake's lair before. To her knowledge, no squirrel ever had. Once she was inside, the hole opened up into a passage large enough for her to walk upright. She kept her firethorns in front of her.

2

Each step down the passage took the brave squirrel deeper into the musky scent of dirt and snake. Deeper and deeper into the darkness. Witch-Hazel's eyes adjusted, and she could see rocky outcroppings and dangling bits of roots in the smoothed dirt walls around her. Eventually, the stink of snake lessened, replaced by unfamiliar eldritch smells—ancient and forgotten. Witch-Hazel had never been this deep beneath the ground before. Squirrels were creatures of the sky. They couldn't fly, but they leapt from branch to branch, free and unhindered.

The dirt walls around Witch-Hazel felt like a snake's coils, wrapping tightly around her, strangling away her freedom. Yet the musical call of the Celestial Fragments and her memory of the snake's enticing song drew her on.

The corridor took a sharp turn, and Witch-Hazel's breath caught when she saw two round glimmers of gold. She froze, too frightened to raise her firethorns, expecting any moment to feel the sharp bite of the snake's fangs followed by deadly poison coursing through her body, burning her from the inside out.

Death didn't come.

Witch-Hazel's broad, fluffy tail flicked in confusion and relief. She looked closer at the circles of gold: they weren't snake eyes; they were two gold medallions embedded in a wooden door blocking her passage deeper into the tunnel. Witch-Hazel tried to open the door, but it wouldn't give. So she looked closer at the medallions.

The two gold medallions had images etched in their yellow surfaces—complicated images. A starburst filled the middle of each medallion, and the many points reached out to the edges. Ringing around the edges were tiny images of animals, all different kinds of animals, positioned at the multitudinous tips of each starburst. Two dozen or more tiny animals were etched in the smooth gold.

Witch-Hazel sheathed her firethorn swords and reached a paw out to touch one of the gold medallions. Its metal was cool against her pawpads. She traced a claw along the lines of the starburst and then around the curved medallion edge. She reached up with her other paw and dug all her claws into the wood around the medallion, trying to pry the gold from the surface of the door, but it wouldn't come away.

One of her paws slipped, and the gold medallion turned, still fixed in the door but rotated. Before the medallion had turned, an etching of an eagle had been at the top of the starburst; now the eagle was ninety degrees to the right, and an etching of a mouse was at the top. She turned the medallion again, moving the eagle all the way to the bottom and bringing an etching of a fox to the top of the starburst.

It was a puzzle, she realized. If she turned both of the medallions the right way, then the door would open. At least, she hoped it would.

Witch-Hazel leaned in close to the gold medallions and carefully examined the animal etchings. The same set of thirty animals graced each of them. Many of the animals were familiar—mouse, sparrow, squirrel, snake, otter, beaver, badger, raccoon, deer. Some of them were strange—one had two humps on its back; another seemed to be a bird, but it had long legs and a sinuous neck unlike any bird she'd ever seen; another had a nose like a snake, flappy ears, and legs like tree stumps. That one was the largest of the animals, so she tried turning the medallion until it was at the top of the starburst. Then she turned the second medallion until the mouse was on top. Smallest and largest.

But when she tried the door, it still didn't move. She reversed the order, placing the mouse on the top of the first medallion and the snake-nosed behemoth at the top of the second medallion, but that made no difference. The door still wouldn't budge.

Witch-Hazel tried a variety of combinations, none of which worked, until she began twisting the medallions randomly out of frustration. That didn't work either.

For a while, Witch-Hazel tried methodically turning the medallions—matching the mouse on the first medallion with each of the thirty animals on the second medallion—but the process was so dreary that she started thinking about turning around and going home.

If she hurried, none of her sisters or brothers would even know that she'd been gone. In fact, she probably didn't have to hurry. The shame of her failed adventure could stay hers alone; Witch-Hazel felt a twinge of sadness at the idea. She wanted her disappearance to be noticed. She wanted to return in glory with the Celestial Fragments. She wanted the snake to be right about her being good at finding things that mattered.

Anger flared in Witch-Hazel's narrow chest. The snake had been in this tunnel; it must have known about the locked door. Why had it put silly ideas of adventure under the earth into her head if her path was to be blocked so soon?

Unless … Had the snake expected her to know the answer to this puzzle? Maybe the answer to the puzzle wasn't arcane or abstract. Maybe it was personal. It was about her. And the snake.

Witch-Hazel turned the first medallion until the etching of the snake was atop the starburst; then she turned the second medallion until the squirrel was on top. The snake had come to her. Snake and squirrel.

Witch-Hazel pushed against the door, and it shifted under her paws. She was so surprised that she nearly fell against it.

Steadying herself, Witch-Hazel passed through the door. On the other side, the air in her whiskers fell still; the sound of her own breathing echoed off walls in the distance. She was standing on the edge of a large room, and the ground beneath her feet was no longer packed dirt but the hard smoothness of stone. Her claws clicked against it.

With another cautious step, one of Witch-Hazel's hind paws caught on the rough cloth handle of an abandoned satchel. She knelt down and opened the fabric folds of the satchel to find a crumpled sheet of parchment and six round stones nestled inside. She lifted one of the stones in her paws, pressed her nose against it, and breathed in the granite smell. It didn't seem special, except for its unusual roundness.

When she put the stone down, however, it clacked against the others, and a spider-webbing of crystal flecks glowed dully on all their surfaces. For a moment, Witch-Hazel thought it was a trick of the darkness, casting illusions in her sun-starved eyes. Squirrels don't have the best night vision, and these tunnels were about as dark as midnight with a waning moon. Then she realized that—

with the light from the stones—she could barely make out the shape of scrawled writing on the parchment. The scrawling was too pale to read in the bare-glimmer of light, but she didn't think she'd imagined it.

Witch-Hazel lifted one of the stones again and clacked it down hard this time. The stone's curved surface burst brightly with specks of crystalline-blue light. Witch-Hazel positioned the parchment so that the blue light shone on its surface, and she read the following words:

"*Congratulations, Clever-Brave Squirrel! You are on the journey of a lifetime—a journey that will define you. I've left six Orbs of Candle Crystal to light your way. Don't overuse them—the fire in the crystal dies out over time, but a Clever-Brave Squirrel, such as you, can surely find the Lost Celestial Treasures with an Abundance of Six. A snake, such as myself, has sought them Many Years in these tunnels and never found them. But the Celestial Fragments are not for snakes. Surely, the Fairy Stories For Kittens told you that. They are for Squirrels. You will find Them. Luck and light, A Snake Who Believes In You.*"

Witch-Hazel dropped the parchment as if the snake's signature could inject her with its venom. Words can be sharper than teeth, but it was too late. The snake's words had already sunk deep into Witch-Hazel's heart. She'd never felt clever or brave or believed-in before. She was always the befuddled follower, barely keeping up with the lessons her siblings and all the other squirrels excelled at.

But wasn't it always the runt, the forgotten one, the clumsiest kitten who couldn't keep up who found the treasure in fairy stories?

And the snake was right—in the fairy stories Witch-Hazel's mother had told, the treasure was never for snakes.

Witch-Hazel picked up the parchment again and felt a flare of perverse warmth. Maybe she was playing a snake's sadistic game, but she felt like it might be the first game she'd ever played that she might actually win. And the prize was worth so much more than any of the chestnut troves or acorn hoards her siblings squabbled over.

Strength, flight, endless breath. Witch-Hazel chanted the words to herself as she tucked the snake's satchel over one shoulder, keeping a single glowing candle crystal in her paw to light the way.

Strength, flight, endless breath. She chanted the words as she crossed the large room to find three arching doorways yawning in the wall on the far side. *Three treasures; three pathways.* But her chanted words didn't help her choose a path. Each doorway looked exactly the same. She sniffed the air, and they all smelled the same too: still and musty.

Witch-Hazel wondered how much the snake knew about the different paths and why it hadn't left her a map. And yet, a map to what? The snake didn't know where the lost treasures were.

"I'll go a little ways down each path, see what's there, and then turn back," Witch-Hazel said to herself. Her chirping voice echoed eerily in the stone-walled room. "Then I'll know better which path to take."

3

Witch-Hazel took the path on the left. Beyond the stone archway, the passage returned to packed dirt walls and flooring. The dirt had been worn smooth, but it was broken up every so often by another stone archway. To measure her progress, Witch-Hazel sang to herself as she skipped along the passageway. The song she chose was a common nut-gathering song.

Acorns and walnuts,
Chestnuts and seeds,
Shining brown fruit of the shrubs and the trees,
Find them, hide them, find them again,
Acorns and walnuts,
Chestnuts and seeds.

Pinecones, mushrooms,
Apples and pears,
Dream all winter until spring is here,
Of eating fresh strawberries.
Pinecones, mushrooms,

Apples and pears.

Pecans, pistachios,
Raspberries like gems,
If you find them, treasure them,
Summer makes these treats for you,
Pecans, pistachios,
And raspberries too.

The song echoed along the tunnel, and Witch-Hazel began to alter the rhythm of the song, causing the echoes to trip along after her own voice, almost like a duet. It was a strangely pleasing effect. Still, after a few repetitions, Witch-Hazel decided it was time to turn back. The path looked like it might stay exactly the same for a long time, and there was a chance that one of the other two paths would lead somewhere more clearly interesting.

Witch-Hazel skipped her way back along the tunnel, singing and counting the stone archways she'd passed, but when she should have reached the stone room where she'd started, it wasn't there. Instead, the path branched in two different directions. She didn't remember passing any forks in the path on her way down …

Confused, Witch-Hazel turned around several times, tilting her head to look at each path from every angle. They looked the same—smooth packed dirt floors, rounded walls. They smelled the same—musty and ancient. The air felt the same—still and cold. And with horror and an involuntary squeak, Witch-Hazel realized that she no longer remembered which direction she'd come from. She didn't know the way back out.

Witch-Hazel knelt down and clacked the candle crystal extra hard against the floor, igniting its sparks of light. The blue glow shone brighter and illuminated the three paths farther down, but they still looked the same.

Maybe if she took a few steps, she'd see farther and the stone room where she'd started would become visible. Still, Witch-Hazel didn't want to get any more lost than she already was, so she set the freshly glowing candle crystal down on the floor, scratched a divot in the dirt to keep it from rolling away, and left it right in the middle of the forking path. She wouldn't get any farther from the fork than she was able to see the blue glow of the candle crystal.

Witch-Hazel edged down one of the three identical paths, glancing back at the blue glow frequently. When she reached a stone archway, she put her paw against it to steady herself and closed her eyes briefly. Her heart was racing out of control at the thought that she might be lost, trapped under the earth.

Squirrels are meant for the wind blowing through branches. Not the still air of a tomb.

Witch-Hazel opened her eyes and turned back to look at the candle crystal but saw only darkness. Turning frantically, she saw nothing. No light. None at all. She grabbed her bushy tail and hugged it tight for comfort.

When Witch-Hazel had her panicked breathing back under control, she reached a paw into the satchel slung over her shoulder with her five remaining candle crystals. She couldn't believe she'd already lost one. She grabbed one of the smooth, round stones and clacked it hard against the wall, bringing the light back.

Now she was twice lost and one candle crystal down. Worse, Witch-Hazel felt a tickling premonition that the passageways down here were rearranging themselves. She'd been very careful, and the stone room where she'd started wasn't where it was supposed to be.

Witch-Hazel smoothed out her tail, twitched it, and let it go. She took a deep breath and straightened the satchel of candle crystals and the knapsack of goodies on her back. No worries. Had she really thought that she could journey deep under the earth to find the missing Celestial Fragments without ever getting lost? She had, but it was a foolish thought. She was on an adventure, and getting lost was part of the deal.

Unsure of which way to go, Witch-Hazel placed her glowing candle crystal on the floor and let it roll, keeping her paws close enough to pick it up again at any moment. The crystal rolled to her left, so that was down—deeper into this dungeon. That was the way she would go.

Witch-Hazel picked the candle crystal up and carried it for as long as it continued to glow, but when the flecks of crystal dimmed and went out, she put it back in the satchel. She could navigate halls like these in the dark.

Whiskers twitching, Witch-Hazel continued down the dirt and stone passageway, singing duets with her echo, and tasting the air carefully for any changes. The echo-duets grew more complicated until Witch-Hazel almost felt like her echo was another squirrel, walking by her side, keeping her company and singing with her. It was a cheerful, friendly feeling, and Witch-Hazel, giddy from the darkness and suppressed terror, decided to play along with it.

When she finished the song, Witch-Hazel said to her new imaginary friend, "Shall we sing a different one next?"

Her heart nearly stopped when her echo answered, "All right. Do you know 'Hills and Trees Yonder'?"

Witch-Hazel couldn't decide between reaching for one of her firethorn swords or one of the candle crystals. In her flustered panic, she reached for both and tangled her arms in the strap of the satchel. All five of the remaining candle crystals spilled out and bounced to the floor where they burst with shining crystalline specks of light.

In the blue glow, Witch-Hazel found herself staring at a reflection of herself but much more tired and ragged than she'd been when she'd entered this snake's dungeon. Here was a squirrel who'd been trapped in the dark for days or weeks, not merely hours—fur rumpled and greasy, clothing torn, and skinny from hunger. For a moment, Witch-Hazel questioned whether the dark passageways were playing with her sense of time as well as her sense of space. Had she been down here months? Starving away? The twisting tunnels had rearranged themselves around her as she walked through them; why not speed the passage of time as well?

Perhaps it truly was a mirror. But when Witch-Hazel reached a paw out, the other squirrel didn't reach back. Instead the second squirrel flinched, stepped backward and giggled, an edge of hysteria in her voice.

"How long have you been down here?" Witch-Hazel asked.

No answer. Only another frightened, hiccoughing giggle.

Witch-Hazel tried a different tack: "What's your name?"

The squirrel hesitated, as if she could hardly remember her own name down here in the dark, and when she did speak, her voice was strange and stilted. "My name's Salal-Berry. I've been here since the snake sang to me."

"The snake sang to me too," Witch-Hazel said. Slowly—so as not to startle Salal-Berry—she leaned down and began gathering the five candle crystals back into her satchel.

"I had candle crystals at first," Salal-Berry said. "I used them up."

"Have you been in the dark since then?" Witch-Hazel asked.

The ragged squirrel's left ear twitched, and one of her paws picked at the other one, pulling out bits of her already thin fur. "You get used to it. Want some mushrooms? I'll show you how to find them ..." Salal-Berry's words trailed off. Her head tilted, and she stared fixedly at the satchel slung over Witch-Hazel's shoulder. "What's in there? I'll trade you mushrooms for what's in there."

"All that's in here is candle crystals, and you don't seem to need those." Witch-Hazel pulled her satchel close under her arm, clutching it against her side.

"What about the pack on your back?" Salal-Berry's nose twitched eagerly, smelling the walnuts and crocus bulbs in Witch-Hazel's knapsack.

"You haven't asked me if I can lead you back out," Witch-Hazel observed, trying not to feel threatened.

The ragged squirrel laughed, a hollow barking sound that echoed down the tunnel. "There is no way out. You're one of the snake's toys now. It can slither through the walls, you know? Appear at will, as if by magic. That serpent will play with you like a spinning acorn in a kitten's paws—spinning, spinning, dizzy, and finally eaten."

"You haven't been eaten."

"But I'm dizzy."

Witch-Hazel couldn't argue with that. She was beginning to feel dizzy too, talking to this shadowy version of herself in a small pool of blue light, deep underground. Faintness flushed her body, and she leaned against the wall to support herself. Maybe she was hungry. "Tell you what," she said. "I have some crocus and tulip bulbs. Show me how to find the mushrooms, and then we can settle down, eat together, and try to figure this all out."

Salal-Berry barked that hollow laugh again, shook her head as if amused, and then wandered off muttering about snakes and tricks, mushrooms and treasures. Witch-Hazel wasn't sure what to do, but then Salal-Berry turned back and beckoned to her. "Aren't you coming?"

So Witch-Hazel scurried along, holding the candle crystal up for light. Although Salal-Berry didn't seem to need it; she had become a creature of the dark. The ragged squirrel let one paw trail along the tunnel wall beside her, and she held the other out in front of her, ready to warn her if the tunnel twisted or turned too suddenly in front of her. Witch-Hazel wondered if she'd become one too before her quest was over. Assuming her quest was ever over. If this ragged squirrel was to be believed, her quest could only end in one of two ways: dying slowly in the dark or dying quickly in the snake's mouth.

Witch-Hazel refused to believe that. She believed she would find the treasure. Maybe it made her a fool, but at least she was a fool on a quest, instead of a fool bumbling around, making mistakes and being laughed at by all the squirrels in the trees of home.

4

COUNTLESS TWISTS AND TURNS LATER, Salal-Berry spun around suddenly to stare Witch-Hazel in the face. Their faces were so close together the eerie squirrel's sour breath stirred Witch-Hazel's whiskers. Her haunted eyes reflected the blue glow of the candle crystal, and in the crystal's light, Witch-Hazel could see that the fur on her face was thin and lined with scars, as if she'd been clawing at herself down here in the dark.

"We're here," Salal-Berry sighed, like the creaking sound of a branch in the wind at night.

"Where?" Witch-Hazel asked, unsure how they could be anywhere specific in this tangle of tunnels. "I thought we were lost. I thought we were looking for mushrooms."

Salal-Berry stepped to the side, and the faint glow of the candle crystal illuminated a bulging hollow in the tunnel behind her. The walls of the tunnel swelled out and up, making a sort of room. Half of the space in the room was filled with broken bits of twig and roots, woven together into a waist-high sloppy nest; the wall on that side was covered with scratchings in the dirt—nothing so coherent as actual writing. More like cryptic runes.

The floor on the other side was covered in scraps of trash or treasure—bits of bone, bits of stone, tufts of fur, and most disturbingly, shed snakeskin. The wall on that side was slick with moisture and vilely orange mushroom shelves grew out of the muddy dirt. Although the mere sight of their vomit-like color was enough to make Witch-Hazel gag, they had all been nibbled on. Their moldy scent filled the air like a thick perfume. Witch-Hazel wondered what toxic fungal poisons were destroying Salal-Berry's body while the snake's games destroyed her mind.

"This is the snake's home for me," Salal-Berry said. "The tunnels always bring me here."

"Always?"

"Whether I delve deeper, looking for the treasures—" Salal-Berry's eyes narrowed and glinted. She hissed the next words: "*You thought I didn't know you were seeking the celestial treasures? You thought you could hide it from me?*" Then her voice returned to normal, as if she'd been possessed. "—or whether I despair and seek the way back out, back to the trees, back to the sky ..." The gleam in her eyes dulled. "No matter. Always here. The tunnels move and writhe around me, always bringing me here. It's where the snake wants me." The hiss returned to her voice, and she said, "*I wonder if it's where the snake wants you.*"

Witch-Hazel still held the candle crystal in one paw, but her free paw strayed to the hilt of one of her firethorn swords. She had never feared a squirrel before. Not truly. She'd squabbled and wrestled over chestnuts and branches. She'd been scratched up. But she'd never wondered before whether another squirrel might kill her. She'd never seen another squirrel so desperate and separated from the rules and strictures of squirrel society.

"I don't do what snakes want," Witch-Hazel said in even, measured tones. "I do what I want."

Salal-Berry's emaciated body doubled over and quaked. Witch-Hazel thought the crazed squirrel was coughing or dying. But then she straightened up enough for Witch-Hazel to see the twinkle in her eyes. Salal-Berry's body was wracked with hilarity, shaking with mad laughter.

When Salal-Berry finally regained her composure, she said, "What a delightful delusion. And you haven't even had a bite of the mushroom yet." She gestured vaguely toward the acid-orange fungus. "It will make you dream. Time will pass faster and slower. Have some. And give me the bulbs." She held out a greedy paw.

Witch-Hazel would never taste that mushroom. She swore to herself, no matter how hungry she got, she wouldn't let it poison her. "No thank you," she said primly, still resting one paw on a firethorn.

Salal-Berry's eyes flashed, and Witch-Hazel tightened her grip on the sword.

"*You promised,*" the crazed squirrel hissed. "*A trade.*"

The weight of Witch-Hazel's knapsack on her back felt like a liability. Something this crazed squirrel wanted to steal. As Witch-Hazel had followed Salal-Berry through the tunnels, she'd sincerely planned to share the tulip and crocus bulbs with her. The poor thing was clearly starved out of her mind. But now ... This no longer felt like sharing. It felt like extortion. It felt like Salal-Berry would leap at her, claws and fangs bared, any moment.

"I didn't promise a trade," Witch-Hazel hedged. "I said we'd share."

"*Then share,*" Salal-Berry hissed. And the crazed squirrel leapt forward.

Witch-Hazel drew a firethorn sword with one paw, but with the other paw, she panicked and hurled the candle crystal at the menace of teeth and claws and fury flying toward her. The ball of stone flew true and pelted Salal-Berry hard in the stomach. The angry squirrel lurched, wrapping one arm around her belly where the stone ball had struck.

Salal-Berry cursed in a hissing tongue. Was it snake-language? Witch-Hazel couldn't be sure. She couldn't focus. Her wooden sword was between her and the crazed squirrel, but Witch-Hazel couldn't bring herself to plunge its dagger-end into the hissing squirrel's heart.

Part of Witch-Hazel—a voice deep inside, the voice that used to tell her to steal from her sisters and brothers and then lie to their mother about it—told her that she'd be putting the pathetic, deranged animal out of its misery. Killing it was the right thing to do.

The kind thing. The merciful thing.

Witch Hazel raised her sword.

The candle crystal, discarded and rolling on the damp floor, flickered out.

In total darkness, Salal-Berry laughed maniacally. Witch-Hazel pointed her sword, trying to track the laughter, but the mocking sound came from all sides. Salal-Berry had become part of the darkness, part of the tunnel, part of the belly of the snake; her voice hissed with its tongue. The tunnels, the snake, the crazed squirrel—they were all one.

Witch-Hazel's heart beat wildly. She drew her second firethorn sword and held each sword out. The laughter grew and echoed until it no longer fit in the chamber; it was crushing Witch-Hazel's soul. She flailed her sharp wooden weapons, stabbing the darkness, fighting the laughter with every ounce of energy she could summon. They struck only air. But Witch-Hazel tripped, and the four candle crystals in her satchel tumbled out, clacked against the floor, and burst to light.

The candle crystals' blue glow—four times as bright as before—revealed Salal-Berry, crouched in her nest, strangely still.

Witch-Hazel didn't hesitate. She thrust her firethorn swords into the other squirrel, skewering her narrow, emaciated chest from either side. The swords crossed each other's paths, a crucifix through the heart of Salal-Berry. Doubly stabbed. Murdered twice over. The laughter stopped. Salal-Berry's eyes went dull.

Witch-Hazel dropped to the floor outside the nest, exhausted, confused, and muttering, "What have I done? What have I done?" She slumped on the damp earth, sobbing to herself, aghast and overcome. It had been so easy. The swords had passed through Salal-Berry's body like the other squirrel was nothing—a mere shade or shadow of the snake's mind games. An echo of Witch-Hazel's own singing voice.

The memory of singing with Salal-Berry curdled and soured in Witch-Hazel's mind. She was a murderer, and a murderer had no right to sing.

Unless it was a eulogy.

Salal-Berry deserved a song to honor her.

Witch-Hazel haltingly pushed herself up from the floor, planning to sing a song over Salal-Berry's bones. A song of sorrow; a song of repentance; a song begging for unworthy, unearned, impossible forgiveness. But when Witch-Hazel looked over the twiggy wall of the nest, there was nothing amidst the shadows inside but bones: a skeleton skewered by two wooden swords, crossing each other inside an empty rib cage. No heart, although it should have been beating only minutes ago. No glassy eyes, staring reproach at Witch-Hazel in their death. Only the empty eye sockets of a bone-white skull. Salal-Berry's fluffy tail had been reduced to a narrow skeletal whip of bones.

Witch-Hazel shuddered, and any strands of memorializing song in her heart dried to dust in her throat.

Somehow in the silence and stillness, the skull still seemed to be laughing at her. Frozen in laughter.

Witch-Hazel was losing her mind. Time meant nothing down here.

Grasping for the stability of mundanity, Witch-Hazel began gathering up the scattered candle crystals from the tunnel floor. It was a simple, routine action—tidying up. She stuffed three of the glowing balls into her satchel. She held the fourth out, lighting the room, as she searched for the candle crystal she'd thrown at Salal-Berry. The light of that fifth crystal had gone out, hidden in one of the dark corners of the room.

Witch-Hazel scoured every corner: beneath the orange shelves of mushroom, under the scraps of fur and dry paper-like snakeskin, around the twiggy edges of Salal-Berry's nest.

The fifth candle crystal was gone. Witch-Hazel was down to four.

Unless … the candle crystal had bounced off of the far wall and landed inside the nest. With Salal-Berry's dry bones.

Witch-Hazel approached the mocking face of her insanity—the death mirror of herself—Salal-Berry's slumped skeleton. Trying not to disturb the bones, Witch-Hazel pulled out one firethorn sword and sheathed it in her belt, then the other. In spite of her care, the skeletal shape of Salal-Berry crumpled, and dry dust exploded in a cloud from the pile of bones.

The shape of a squirrel was gone; all that was left was the mocking skull and a jumble of bones. The squirrel itself had gone long ago—before Witch-Hazel had entered this labyrinth of darkness, before she'd ever heard the snake sing. The bones were not Salal-Berry. Perhaps, Salal-Berry had never existed at all.

The bones were *not* her.

But the skull wouldn't stop laughing at her. Witch-Hazel reached into the nest, grabbed the skull and shoved it in the satchel with the candle crystals, so it would stop staring at her.

Witch-Hazel needed to pull herself together. And she needed all of the candle crystals to escape this labyrinth of madness. So, she crawled over the nest's wall to truly search inside it. Her feet crunched against the shifting surface of twigs and bones. Gritting her teeth, imagining that she was back in her own poorly made nest, looking for something she'd lost—nothing more, nothing sinister, nothing unusual—she reached into the remaining pile of bones with her paw, searching by touch for the smooth, stony feel of a candle crystal.

Instead, she felt a draft, as if the nest were breathing. A deep, contented sigh passed through the room. Witch-Hazel shivered, her gray fur prickling, and her head cleared a little with the fresh scent of clean air. Old air. Stale air. But not tainted by the thick stink of the orange mushrooms.

If the air was moving up through the nest, there was an empty space underneath. Witch-Hazel clambered out and began disassembling the nest, pulling out one clump of twigs after another, destroying the nest's loose weave, and shoving the twigs to the far side of the room, the damp, mushroomy side.

Once the nest was half cleared away, the pile of bones inside clattered down, but they didn't fall on a damp dirt floor. They fell, echoing, into a rocky, craggy tunnel entrance, still half-hidden by the nest.

Witch-Hazel stared at the tunnel entrance in wonder. Had Salal-Berry been hiding it from her? Or hiding it from herself? Or … had she led Witch-Hazel here … to complete the next step in a quest that had broken her?

Assuming Salal-Berry had ever existed and wasn't simply a phantom hallucination of the darkness and fungal fumes.

It didn't matter. Whatever had brought Witch-Hazel here, she was here now. And the cool air rising out of the tunnel, sighing against her fur, called to her. This was the way she was meant to go.

5

Witch-Hazel cleared away the rest of the twiggy nest and clambered into the narrow, rocky passageway that had been hidden beneath it. She couldn't hold a candle crystal ahead of her for light—she needed all four of her paws to navigate the irregular bumps and boulders, squeezing her way down, down, down. She barely fit. Rocks pressed against her from above, flattening her ears and bruising her hunched back when she wasn't careful. Being surrounded on every side, hugged tightly by rocks, was a claustrophobic feeling for a creature of treetops.

Witch-Hazel tried to pretend she was hiding inside the hollow heart of a dead tree snag, playing a simple game of hide-and-seek with her siblings. A kitten again. Carefree. It didn't work well. Every time she bumped her head, it felt like a rock had been thrown at her. The imaginary tree snag was filling with pebbles, drowning her under rock, burying her alive. *Why were her siblings throwing rocks at her? What had she done wrong?*

They didn't know she was a murderer. At least … not yet.

Or was she?

Witch-Hazel shook her arboreal imaginings from her head. Her game of pretend was only making the climb worse.

And she could no longer sing to pass the time. Not after her ghostly duets with Salal-Berry. And yet, she heard the unearthly strands of a song echoing in her head, giving a rhythm to her downward trek. After a while, she hummed along. She wouldn't sing, but she could hum.

The song became familiar. She'd heard its rhythms and musical inflections before … It was the snake's song, but the voice was different. Instead of a sliver-thin hiss, this voice was full and resonant. It rumbled in the stone, telling the story of the All-Being and the lost Celestial Fragments at the edge of Witch-Hazel's hearing.

The tight, rocky passageway opened up gradually until Witch-Hazel realized she could stand upright again. The air sighed around her, and Witch-Hazel noticed that she could see her paws feeling the way in front of her, finding her way through the passage. That meant there was light. Deep underground, there was light.

Witch-Hazel sniffed the air carefully, but the stench of the orange mushrooms was gone. This wasn't a hallucination. At least, she didn't think so.

A little farther down the passage, she saw twisting lines of green light crawling across her vision. It almost looked like the patterns she saw when she closed her eyes, mere tricks of the darkness. But then the air in her whiskers changed so dramatically, she came to a sudden stop, afraid to take a single step more.

Slowly, Witch-Hazel's eyes adjusted to what she was seeing. The darkness ahead of her was no longer close by. She was standing on the edge of an empty chasm—a cavern large enough to hold all of her family's trees, from roots to sky-high leaves. The light came from lichen on the rocks of the ceiling where constellations of green glowed like a starry sky. Far beneath, the stone had been carved into a labyrinth. Half circles and parallel lines, stone walls encircling stone walls—all of them too widely apart for a squirrel to jump from the top of one wall to the next. The maze would have to be navigated by its own rules without shortcuts. In the center, a wide round dais, surrounded by enough dead-ends to drive a squirrel mad.

A voice very close to Witch-Hazel rumbled, "It's beautiful, isn't it?" It was the voice that had been singing before.

Witch-Hazel looked around, but she didn't see anyone who could have spoken. She wasn't sure she wanted to meet anyone else down here. Especially not the owner of such a deep, rumbling voice—such a creature must be very large and intimidating. Witch-Hazel's fur prickled, but since she couldn't see the creature, she didn't know which way to run.

The voice spoke again, deep and booming, "An ancient mole king had his subjects build this labyrinth to protect his treasure."

In spite of herself, Witch-Hazel's attention was drawn away from the dangerous voice and to the sight of the labyrinth stretched out below her. Her gaze followed one line of stone after another, trying to trace a path to the center. Every one of the paths came to a dead end. Or else Witch-Hazel's eyes lost track of the lines of gray on gray in the dark. "It's a trap," Witch-Hazel said carefully. "There must be a trick to it. Whoever knows the trick can get to the center." She looked around herself again, searching for a face somewhere near her in the dark. "Do you know the trick?"

The face of a mountain lion resolved out of the darkness, right beside the little squirrel—a monster at her shoulder. The monster spoke: "I am the trick." The lioness's face alone was almost as large as Witch-Hazel's entire body. Her tawny muzzle split in an enigmatic smile—half toothy threat and half friendly solicitation.

Witch-Hazel hadn't come this far to become a mouth-sized morsel. The nerves in her body screamed for her to run. Yet the lioness could have already eaten her by now, if she'd wanted to. The lioness's gold eyes twinkled in a way that was playful but not unkind.

The small squirrel puffed out her chest and held her ground. Though her paws drifted to the hilts of the firethorn swords at her waist. "You're the sphinx who guards the mole king's lost treasure with a riddle?" Witch-Hazel had heard of the sphinx and Great Pyramids. Even squirrels tell tales of the great treasures of the world—stories passed to them from migratory birds, passed from one bird to another, across the continents. "Then have at it. Ask me your riddle."

The lioness's face rose higher as the giant creature stepped forward on the rocky ledge beside Witch-Hazel. Her body resolved in shades of gray in the darkness—her head rose from a long slender neck that sprouted out of narrow shoulders, leading into a pair of delicately crossed human arms. She had a human woman's torso, but beneath it was an entire four-legged lion's body, complete with a swishing, tufted tail. "I am a kind of sphinx," the creature said. "Sister to the sphinx, precisely. My sister who was celebrated in Greece and Egypt usually claims the name. I am less well-known. I am a leontaur, and I don't ask riddles."

Witch-Hazel looked up doubtfully at the lion-creature looming over her. If she were at home in her tree, Witch-Hazel would hide among the highest branches until a creature like this leontaur were gone. Instead, she was dealing with the leonine creature face to face. "Will you show me the way to the center of the maze?" she asked, paws still on sword hilts.

"Gladly." The leontaur's answering grin was toothier than Witch-Hazel liked, but at least the teeth weren't so close now. "Hop astride my back, little one. I will take you to the mole king's treasure. We can talk along the way."

Taking her life into her paws, Witch-Hazel sprang from the floor of the rocky ledge and landed squarely on the leontaur's broad, tawny-furred lion back, at the base of her smooth-skinned human back. At least, Witch-Hazel was far away from the leontaur's leonine fangs and claws. All the sharp bits pointed away from her now.

As the leontaur walked along the tops of the stone walls, following a wending path through the maze with deep pits on either side of her, she told the story of King Wendall William Warson the 31st. A near-sighted, short-statured mole—more mole than most moles. He'd destroyed his kingdom, sending all of his subjects on treasure quests and turning the entire civilian population to the work of mining diamonds and crafting this labyrinth. He'd worked them to death and revolution. His kingdom had torn itself apart, leaving him alone on a pile of treasure in the middle of a maze.

The leontaur's softly rumbling voice, telling its sing-song story, lulled Witch-Hazel to sleep, curled up on a warm bed of tawny fur. In her sleep, the sing-song story words mixed with her dreams. Greedy moles fought with angry moles. Eons of war passed as moles wrestled, gold coins and colorful gemstones raining around them. She was a mole; then she was a squirrel. Treasure weighed her down, dragging her deep into the Earth, clawing at the walls of the bottomless pits of the labyrinth.

Witch-Hazel awoke with a start when the easy gait of the leontaur's steps halted. Even awake, she was still deep under the Earth. The twisted visages of her dreams, angry and snarling, were replaced with a different horror: rows of decapitated mole skulls stuck on spears leered at her from either side of a heap of gold coins, blood-red rubies, and diamonds that glittered like tears. In the center of the pile of treasure, an entire mole skeleton sat on a gold, copper, and silver throne. An emerald-topped silver scepter was still gripped tightly in his skeletal hand, and his skull stared at her like a challenge from beneath a circlet of gold and rubies.

"Why must there be so many skulls?" Witch-Hazel muttered, wiping at the sleep in her eyes. Hoping she was still dreaming. Wondering if her entire journey was a dream and the snake's song had been a lullaby. She'd never seen a dead body before beginning this journey, let alone a skeleton. Now skulls were becoming commonplace.

"These are King Wendall's honor guard," the leontaur answered, gesturing at the rows of skulls with a human hand. Then she pointed at the skeleton on the throne. "That's King Wendall." The leontaur crossed her human arms over her chest and settled down on her haunches, causing Witch-Hazel to slide off her furry back and plop down on the cold stone of the dais.

The leontaur lifted one of her leonine forepaws and lazily licked it, cleaning her razor sharp claws—displaying her lethality. "If you want a portion of King Wendall's treasure, ask him for it."

"Ask the skeleton?" Witch-Hazel backed cautiously away from the leontaur, incredulous. The gold and gems were guarded by nothing more than the decapitated heads of dead moles; she could stuff her knapsack full, and their bones could only watch. Although … Salal-Berry had been only bones too, in the end.

Besides, the leontaur had promised a trick.

Even if the dead king didn't spring to eerily animated un-life to defend his treasure, the leontaur could defend it with a single swipe of her giant paw.

Perhaps, if Witch-Hazel wasn't polite to the skeleton, the leontaur would punish her. Then again, the leontaur might punish Witch-Hazel no matter what she did. Cats were notorious for torturing their prey—much more so than snakes. And human arms and torso aside, the leontaur was a lion. A big cat. And Witch-Hazel had let that big cat bring her to the middle of a maze.

"I didn't come here for gold and rubies …" Witch-Hazel mused to herself. They wouldn't be worth anything to her back home. Chestnuts and acorns were more valuable than metal and stones. No matter how pretty, these baubles weren't valuable enough to have drawn her by the treacherous voices of snakes and cats to this dark depth under the earth. "I came down here for the Celestial Fragments. I don't need Earthly treasures, fruits of the cold ground. I want to meet the All-Being, not weigh myself down with worthless riches."

The leontaur tilted her head, intrigued, and her dilated golden eyes sparkled. "And here I thought you slept through my lesson. Yet you understood the moral anyway. Clever squirrel."

Witch-Hazel was torn between feeling flattered and patronized. Either way, her paws moved back to the hilts of her firethorn swords. They'd be little use against a full-sized lion, sphinx-like or not. But they gave her comfort.

"Regardless," the leontaur rumbled laconically, "you've learned your lesson too late." She lay down on her lion's side, beside the pile of treasure, and her human hand reached out to caress the gold coins. She traced loving patterns over the dimpled surface of coins and gems with her delicate, long fingers. With a vicious, toothy grin, the leontaur picked up a single blood-red ruby and clenched it tight inside her human fist.

The stone ground shook under Witch-Hazel's hind paws, and she stumbled. Laughter erupted from all around her. The earthquake itself felt like the ground laughing, but it was worse than that: the bone-dead mole skulls laughed maniacally from their wooden stakes, naked jawbones wagging.

The skeleton of King Wendall William Warson the 31st rose from its ornate throne and pointed its silver-and-emerald scepter at Witch-Hazel. "Usurper!" the skeleton cried, voice rattling like dry bones. "Thief!"

"But, but …" Witch-Hazel stuttered at the mole skeleton. She wasn't the one who'd stolen a ruby! The shock of it all robbed her of the ability to find words. Finally, she settled on wordlessly pointing one of her firethorn swords at the leontaur's clenched fist.

The leontaur threw the ruby at Witch-Hazel, and it bounced sharply off her gray tufted ear. "You think King Wendall would turn on me? I've been one of his loyal guards for millennia. Since long before your grandmother's grandmother ever hid a nut."

Witch-Hazel sputtered irately and incoherently at this unfairness.

The leontaur shrugged her narrow human shoulders and purred, "What can I say? It's dull guarding an abandoned pile of gold in a dank dungeon. Much more fun to watch a plucky squirrel adventurer fight mole spirits for her life!"

The leontaur's words sent a shiver down Witch-Hazel's spine. Her bushy tail whipped wildly. She drew her second firethorn sword and looked around to see swirling fog condensing around the laughing mole skulls.

The fog formed into the translucent shape of a spirit mole around each skull. The spirit-moles straightened up, lifting their skulls off of the wooden pikes that had held them. The moles were smaller than Witch-Hazel, but there were a lot of them, nearly two dozen. Once they were corporeal enough, each mole turned around and grabbed its wooden pike, arming itself. Wisps of fog trailed away from the moles as they moved. Their bony white skulls and empty eye sockets stared out through the unearthly spiritual visages formed by the fog. Translucent, smoky mole faces with dead skulls behind them.

6

WITCH-HAZEL SQUARED HERSELF for battle, holding one firethorn sword toward each row of cackling spirit-moles. "I don't want your filthy gold and rubies!" she squeaked. She'd meant to sound more certain, more threatening. Instead, she sounded like what she was: a small, scared squirrel with no trees to scurry into, far out of her element.

"You've come here to insult me then?!" King Wendall rattled, adjusting the golden crown on his skull with skeletal fingers. His skeleton had become cloaked in a foggy spirit body as well, but his bones shone through eerily. "Death to thieves! Death to infidels!" He swept his emerald scepter broadly in front of him, like a conductor leading a ghostly orchestra. "Honor Guard, attack!"

Witch-Hazel took a step backward, but she couldn't take many more. The dais with the treasure was surrounded by a deep pit, too steep to climb—if she fell into it, she might never find her way back out. And that was if she survived the fall.

Four narrow stone paths led away from the dais, but she couldn't remember which of them the leontaur had brought her along. Even if she could, she had slept through most of the journey, and she wouldn't know the way back through the maze. Especially not with ghostly moles chasing her.

She had to fight.

The ghostly moles advanced on Witch-Hazel from either side. They lowered their pikes, and the closest mole hunched its ghostly shoulders, leaned in, and rushed upon her.

What she lacked in practice and training, Witch-Hazel made up for in adrenaline-fueled enthusiasm: she swung one firethorn sword clumsily at the mole's pike, whacking it hard, and thrust the other sword through the mole's wispy spirit body. The sword passed harmlessly through the dark fog, slashing a swirling gap in the misty body that simply filled back in moments later.

Two more spirit-moles charged with their pikes. Witch-Hazel was too shocked by the ineffectual nature of her attack to properly defend herself, but she lucked into dodging the moles' pointed wooden weapons by tripping over her own foot. One of the pikes stabbed through the long, fine hair of her bushy tail, as harmlessly as her own sword had passed through the fog. The other pike rammed into the stone ground beside Witch-Hazel with a resounding CLACK. The moles were small and wispy, but they were strong.

Witch-Hazel rolled away from the pike's pointed end, but her satchel's strap was caught around it. She shrugged her shoulder out of the strap, leaving the bag of candle crystals behind. She got her feet under her and sprang up, now completely surrounded by spirit-moles.

"Swear fealty to me," King Wendall rattled from his throne, "and you can join my Honor Guard—your skull will look upon my gleaming treasure for all eternity! Can you think of anything more utopian?"

Witch-Hazel's thoughts strayed back to home. *Swaying tree branches. A cool spring breeze. Daffodils dancing like yellow stars.* The world she'd left behind—full of trees and family, overbearing but loving—was much more of a utopia than this dark underground lair.

"Yes!" Witch-Hazel squeaked. "This is no utopia! Dead moles and cold gold do not a utopia make!"

Witch-Hazel swung the firethorn sword in her right paw with all her energy. The long narrow wooden blade sliced harmlessly through the foggy torso of the nearest mole, but it kept swinging, and Witch-Hazel kept spinning, slicing upward. The firethorn sword continued on to the next spirit-mole where it sliced through the undead creature's foggy facade … but under the smoky snarling face, the wooden blade made contact: it whacked into the one solid part of the mole's sepulchral body—its bone-white skull.

The mole's skull flew through the air; its cloudy spirit-body streaked after it like a comet's tail. The mole's angry face stretched out in a cosmic scream as it soared away from the treasure dais, leaving too little of its foggy body behind to hold onto its weapon. The pike clattered to the stone floor, abandoned, and then the entire ghostly being disappeared into the dim grayness of the maze. A few moments later, a bouncing crash echoed through the cavern.

Witch-Hazel hoped to high heaven that she was hearing the sound of that demonic skull shattering into bits. Then she instantly regretted her thought as she pictured the ghost mole returning to her as a cloud of bone chips. She needed to get out of here before that ghost mole could find its way back. At least the game had changed. She knew how to fight the remaining ghost moles.

Witch-Hazel whirled like a tornado around the treasure dais, one firethorn sword in each paw, whacking every last ghost mole in the skull. A few of them jabbed her with their pikes—she took a glancing blow to her side and a sharp blow to her left paw—but she kept fighting through the pain, whacking at the moles' skulls, until all of King Wendall's honor guard had flown away into the darkness like a meteor shower of the undead.

Leaving only King Wendall William Warson the 31st himself, standing in front of his throne on a pile of treasure. His ghostly cloud body was more solidly anchored to an entire, intact skeleton, but he was still nothing more than smoke and bones.

"Is that all you've got?" Witch-Hazel laughed at the furious ghost king. Her bushy tail flicked and flipped wildly. Her whole body quivered, giddy from adrenaline.

"Overconfident," the leontaur purred, rolling onto her side like a playful kitten. She batted one lion's paw lazily at a few gold coins on the stone floor. "Take her down, Wendall."

King Wendall ground his teeth together, and his ghostly facade sneered. He raised his scepter and rushed Witch-Hazel. Even made from bones and fog, the mole king had powerful shoulders, and the squirrel was still panting heavily from her battle with his honor guard. The silver-and-emerald scepter came down hard between her ears, and King Wendall grabbed her throat with a bony paw.

Witch-Hazel sputtered and gasped while the mole king squeezed. He was too close for her long swords to do any good. She dropped them and pried at the bony paw, trying to free her throat.

"You still need air to fight?" King Wendall sneered. "I'll cure you of that!" He dropped his silver scepter and squeezed the squirrel's throat two-pawed.

Witch-Hazel couldn't pry his bony paws away, but she thought that she could grab his treasured scepter from where he'd dropped it on the ground. She felt around until her paw found it; then with her remaining strength, she flung the scepter away from them, gambling that it was more use to her as a lure than a bludgeon. Her throw must have been good, because the pit around the dais echoed with the sound of the scepter bouncing off the stony wall on the beginning of a long fall into the pit of the maze.

King Wendall released Witch-Hazel's neck, and her shoulders thudded down to the floor. A moment more and she would have passed out. Instead, she gasped painfully for air through her bruised throat.

"What have you done!?!" King Wendall screamed in his rattling voice. He crawled to the edge of the dais and looked over the edge, searching for his fallen scepter, but its silver-and-emerald glory was long gone.

Witch-Hazel lifted herself up on a shaky paw. The sight of King Wendall perched so precariously close to the edge of the dais was tempting, but his hold on her neck had been strong, and she was still gasping like a fish out of water. She didn't think she could push the skeletal mole, small though he was, over the edge and into the pit.

But she could throw more of his treasure down.

Witch-Hazel scooted backward over the stone, dragging her bushy tail, until she could reach a fistful of treasure. Her side ached from where one of the honor guard's pikes had hit her, and she had a splitting headache from the scepter's blow. Her left paw was bleeding and left a trail of red smears on the rock. But she grabbed a fistful of gold coins and a ruby; she chucked them through the air towards the nearest edge of the dais, beside King Wendall's hunched skeleton.

The gold coins bounced across the stone, making pinging sounds, and the ruby rolled like a teardrop of blood, crying its way toward the cliff's edge. Witch-Hazel threw more and more fistfuls of treasure, making gold and gems rain down on the stone; most of them didn't make it as far as the edge, but enough of them clattered over to make King Wendall shriek his rattling death-cry again.

"You will pay with years of servitude!" King Wendall screamed, rising from the edge of the dais to approach the desperate squirrel.

Witch-Hazel threw one last fistful of treasure before scooting backward onto the sliding pile of coins, feeling about for any weapons hidden among the gold, diamonds, and rubies. Her own swords lay abandoned on the stone floor, far too close to the menacing mole king. He was stronger than she was; he didn't need air; for all she knew, he couldn't feel pain, except for the pang of loss over his treasure.

That gave Witch-Hazel an idea: she couldn't find a weapon amongst the treasure, but maybe there were delicate trophies she could break. If she couldn't beat the mole king, at least she could torture him with the last of her life. Witch-Hazel scanned the heap of glitters and gleams, frantically searching for anything breakable. Most of the treasure was coins, gem stones, rings, and other small works of jewelry, but at the foot of King Wendall's ornate throne, there sat a bulbous glass bottle, filled with a potion that flickered like a dim fire or an opal reflecting sunlight.

Witch-Hazel scrambled over the sliding pile of treasure, grabbed the bottle with her bleeding paw, and held it high above her pointed ears. "I'll break this!" she squeaked. "So help me, if you advance any closer, I'll shatter its glass on your worthless rubbish pile of gold!"

The skeleton-filled ghost hesitated. Tendrils of smoke swirled around his thick bony fingers as he clasped his dead paws together. "You think that's valuable?" he asked.

Witch-Hazel held the bottle up, tilted it, and watched the opalescent liquid slosh inside. She had no idea if it was valuable. She had no idea what it was. But King Wendall was no longer advancing on her. "Threatening to break it stopped you dead in your tracks, didn't it?" she taunted.

Skulls can't smile and empty eye sockets can't twinkle. But King Wendall's ghostly facade twisted in a mischievous smirk. He was up to something. "If you think it's valuable," his voice clacked, "would you like to trade for it?"

Witch-Hazel frowned at the glass bottle. Apparently, King Wendall wanted to get rid of it. "I didn't say it was valuable *to me*. What is it, anyway? Some kind of curse?"

"Actually," the leontaur purred, still spectating the conflict from her laconic pose, "it's a blessing."

"A blessing I don't want!" King Wendall clacked angrily at the leontaur. Then turning back to the squirrel, his ghostly face warmed into an eerie smile over hard bone. "I mean, of course I want it, but you've shown such … ingenuity … and … bravery …" It was clearly hard for the mole king to praise Witch-Hazel, even as a ruse. "You've earned a boon, and I'll trade that blessing to you for …"

King Wendall shuffled over to where Witch-Hazel had dropped her satchel of candle crystals earlier. He reached into the satchel with heavy-boned paws and pulled out one of the spherical stones. Witch-Hazel didn't want to trade those. She'd need them if she survived.

"Rocks?" King Wendall clacked. "This is what squirrels collect when they venture into a mole's domain?"

Witch-Hazel was relieved that he didn't recognize the candle crystal's value. But then he dropped it on the stone floor and poured out the rest of the contents of the satchel: all four candle crystals burst into blue-flecked light.

"That's more like it!" King Wendall rattled.

Witch-Hazel's stomach turned sour as King Wendall reached down, but he didn't pick up one of the candle crystals. He grabbed a dull white object that had fallen between them: the skull of Salal-Berry.

King Wendall held the skull in front of his face. Its jaw swung open, almost as if Wendall were working the squirrel skull like a morbid hand puppet. "You will make a fine member of my honor guard," he said.

Witch-Hazel didn't want Salal-Berry's skull, but she didn't especially want to trade it to King Wendall either. Salal-Berry had viciously, crazily attacked her—but no squirrel deserved to spend eternity as a ghost slave to this mad king. "No trade," she chittered.

King Wendall's ghostly visage twisted with rage, and he threw the squirrel skull into the pit. "Fine," he snarled. "Then trade for your life. You can have that bottle, but only if you take it far, far away from here."

"That makes no sense!" Witch-Hazel chittered. She didn't want the bottle, whether it was a curse or a blessing. She didn't want King Wendall's madness or the leontaur's riddles disguised as lessons. She'd come down into the dark for revelations and the connectedness of all beings. Instead, skeletons and ghosts cavorted with each other, fighting over scraps of shiny metal and her pack of food that couldn't possibly do their empty exposed rib cages any good.

In a fit of anger, Witch-Hazel threw the opalescent bottle down on the pile of gold. Its glass curves shattered into a sprinkling shower of tiny shards, and the opalescent liquid dripped over the gold coins. Suddenly, Witch-Hazel realized with horror that she was looking for an opal—the

Moon Opal. Could that have been it? Had she destroyed the very treasure she'd come looking for?

The opalescent puddle fizzed and flared, rising up as half smoke, half fire, and filled with dancing colors. From inside the diaspora of flames, a form coalesced—a sinuous squiggle of a body, waist-high to Witch-Hazel, with a spade-shaped head, long tail, and tiny limbs. A salamander. As the flames cleared, the figure's maroon skin gleamed and glistened like it was wet.

Surely, the Moon Opal wouldn't behave this way. Whatever this was, it was not a Celestial Fragment.

"My gold!" the salamander exclaimed, clapping her tiny hands, and wiggling her long body like a string blowing in the breeze. "You've finally finished gathering it."

Witch-Hazel blinked and looked down at the shards of glass sprinkled over the pile of gold. "Were you trapped inside the bottle?" she asked, trying to figure out what to make of this strange salamander. "Are you … are you a genie? Do I get three wishes?"

The leontaur purred in deep amusement, and the salamander laughed with a voice that sounded like water splashing over a pebbly streambed.

Witch-Hazel's pointed ears flattened in irritation, and her tail flicked. She was not a joke. "Why is that funny?" she demanded.

The leontaur purred and introduced the salamander, "This is Queen Amalah." She bowed her leonine head at the tiny queen, barely the size of one of the leontaur's human fingers, and the queen nodded back. "The bottle was a signal flare, nothing more."

"You summoned me here," Queen Amalah said in her babbling-brook voice. She knelt down, her body bending flexuously, and lifted an ornate gold and pearl necklace on a single finger. She placed it around her neck, wrapping it several times so it wouldn't drag on the ground, then continued searching the treasure pile for jewelry to pile on her sinuous little body.

King Wendall didn't object. He was too busy rattling, bones literally shaking inside his wispy ghost shell. All his bravado was gone. The mole king was afraid of this tiny salamander queen.

Once Queen Amalah was done draping her slick body with gold and jewels—she wore rings on every finger, a dozen golden necklaces, and two gem-encrusted crowns balanced on her spade-shaped head—she straightened up and faced the mole king. "Your work is done, Wendall." She waved a jewelry-heavy hand, as if she were brushing away Wendall's cares and fears. "Rest now."

A flash of heat rolled over the dais like thunder. King Wendall William Warson the 31st's ghostly shell dissipated like a bad dream. Mere smoke on the wind. And his bones clattered into a pile on the cold stone floor.

7

When a squirrel freezes, still as stone, like a statue without the slightest twitch in her ears or flick of her tail, it's like time itself has paused. Witch-Hazel felt her heart beating and her own ragged breathing. The rest of the world around her was nothing more than darkness and echoes for the longest time. Eventually, murmurs and then quiet conversation broke into her perception.

The leontaur and salamander queen were talking like old friends.

"What will you do now?" Queen Amalah asked, from where she lounged on the palm of the leontaur's left human hand, still draped in gold and jewels.

"I've heard rumors of an armadillo philosopher in South America," the leontaur purred at the maroon squiggle of an animal on her palm. "Something about building a knighthood in protection of the intrinsic honor of all animals?"

"Oh, yes." The salamander fiddled with one of her many necklaces. "The Philosopher-King, he's calling himself. But I still think of him as Josephor the Fool."

"His knights could probably use an enigmatic foil, so I was thinking of moving down to Colombia and setting up camp there now that Wendall's gone. How's life in the fire realm?"

The salamander queen held out one of her hands to admire the half-dozen rings she'd jammed onto her bulbous fingers. "Eh, only lukewarm." Queen Amalah looked over at Witch-Hazel, and suddenly the squirrel felt like fire shot down her back. "Do you think this squirrel adventurer would make a good handmaiden? I could use a new handmaiden, and I don't know of any other squirrels in the fire realm. She'd be very novel."

Witch-Hazel shuddered at the idea of living in a fire realm. She imagined scorched fur and crackling tree limbs breaking in a spray of embers when she jumped to them. The image was even worse than this underworld.

The leontaur turned her giant golden eyes toward the quivering squirrel and said, "This is one of the snake's conscripts. She has a quest."

Queen Amalah's long tail draped off of the leontaur's palm and curled into an upside down question mark. "Oh? And she's made it this far?"

"She even rejected King Wendall's treasure."

"Did she now?" The salamander queen clambered down from the leontaur's palm and sauntered over to Witch-Hazel. As she walked, her long spine swayed like a willow branch in the breeze. "You don't want gold?" The salamander had to look up to stare Witch-Hazel in the eye, but she still managed to be intimidating. She might be tiny, but this salamander was a queen and possibly a fire sorceress.

Pulling herself together, Witch-Hazel stuttered, "N-no, I don't. And I won't go to your fire realm either."

Queen Amalah's wide mouth curved into a superior smile. "Is that so?" The salamander raised her hands and wiggled her fingers, jingling their many rings, and a wave of fire rose up around her and Witch-Hazel. In the flames, images of salamanders, lizards, fierce birds, praying mantises, scorpions, and other strange insects danced and twirled as if they were at a ball. Behind the fiery dancers, tables were laid out with a feast—bowls of roasted crickets, platters of fruit and nut breads, seed cakes, plump caterpillars on crackers, and rich egg casseroles.

A wave of warm air carried a delicious spicy aroma to Witch-Hazel, and her nose twitched eagerly in spite of herself.

"You may not know it," Queen Amalah said, "but squirrels are creatures of fire, too. Look at how your tail dances—" The salamander pointed around Witch-Hazel at her tail which had begun twitching and waving like a flag on a wildly windy day unbidden. "So like a flame! You are one of my own. Join me."

Witch-Hazel watched mesmerized as the dancers on the curtain of flame bowed to one another, traded partners, laughed, and filled plates with treats from the tables. It was appealing. Handmaiden to the queen would be a prestigious position, wouldn't it? Yet it all felt unbalanced. Where was the water? The creatures of earth and air? She was seeing only a portion of the world through this lens of fire, and she had come down here to learn about all of the world, tied up together, twisted into a braid—not a single fractured piece of it.

"You can't be tempted, can you?" Queen Amalah said the words with pleasure and amazement.

The salamander swept her hands down, and the curtain of flame blew out, leaving a ring of smoke around them. The smoke stung Witch-Hazel's eyes. She blinked at the sudden darkness as her eyes readjusted to the soft green light from the lichen far above on the cave's ceiling.

"Do you think the snake has found a champion who will finally succeed?" the leontaur rumbled.

"Not a chance," the salamander queen answered. "The snake's dreams are nothing but mist in the morning. Phantoms that melt away, leaving a wet chill behind. Nonetheless ..." The salamander queen waddled over to the treasure pile and dug through the gold coins, many of them larger than her head, until she found a particular gold chain. She pulled the chain out of the pile. It swung hypnotically. The gold chain was almost as long as the salamander queen was tall; at its end hung a golden pendant with a many-faceted topaz sparkling in the center. The gold setting around the topaz was shaped like petals, and the piece overall looked like a sunflower. Even in the dull green twilight of the cave, the topaz flashed like a piece of sunlight frozen solid.

"Beautiful," Witch-Hazel breathed. Her tail twitched excitedly, betraying her. The sunflower pendant called to her, singing with sunlight, even if it was merely a distraction from her true quest. "But I can't be bought."

Queen Amalah approached Witch-Hazel, continuing to swing the golden pendant. "I have no intention of buying you." She balled the chain up in her ring-encrusted hands, reached out, and then pressed it into Witch-Hazel's paw. "I've decided to assist you, and this pendant has magical powers. Take it."

Witch-Hazel hesitated a moment longer, and then she wrapped her paws around the slithering gold chain.

"Wear it," the salamander queen pressed. "You must keep it safe."

"What are its powers?" Witch-Hazel asked, uncertain at the idea of hanging a magical pendant with unknown powers around her neck.

"You'll discover them," Queen Amalah said, "only when you need them."

"When a queen bestows a favor on you," the lcontaur rumbled, "*take it.*"

Witch-Hazel shrugged. The sunflower pendant couldn't be any more dangerous than an undead mole king, and she'd survived her battle with him.

She stretched the gold chain out between her paws, lifted it over her pointed ears, and settled it around her neck. The sunflower pendant pressed down warmly against her gray fur, and a tingle of electricity shot through her body from the place where it touched her out to the tips of her toes, her ears, and the quivering end of her tail. She smelled summer grass and blackberry brambles, and in her peripheral vision, she could have sworn she saw the bobbing heads of sunflowers, many times taller than her, swaying in a breeze that she couldn't feel in the dead air of the cave. But when she turned her head, there was nothing there.

Witch-Hazel turned back to thank the queen, but before she could say a word, the salamander winked at her, held a maroon finger sporting three different rings up to her wide lips, and began spinning around like a willow twig caught in a whirlpool in the eddies of a stream. After three turns, orange flames flicked out of her slick maroon skin, and the nearest gold coins lifted off the stone floor, hovered shakily, and spun around the queen.

More and more coins and gems lifted up from the pile of treasure and spun shakily through the air, following the salamander queen's motion, faster and faster, until she was lost in a tornado of gold, diamonds, and rubies.

Witch-Hazel backed away, but the zipping pieces of metal and precious stone flying through the air carefully avoided her and the crouching form of the leontaur.

Finally, King Wendall's ornate throne itself wobbled and lifted into the air to spin around in the tornado of gold. Then in a blink of an eye, the entire treasure trove was gone, and the air stood still. It was as if the stone dais had been an empty expanse all along, and everything—mole ghosts, treasure, and salamander queen—had been nothing more than a hallucination.

Except for the weight of the sunflower pendant resting on Witch-Hazel's breast. She touched it with a paw, tracing its edges with a claw, to assure herself it had all been real. She was afraid of losing her mind down here in the dark caverns of the underworld.

Witch-Hazel gathered up her satchel and candle crystals from where they lay discarded on the edge of the empty dais. She could only find three of the round stones. One must have been knocked over the edge during Queen Amalah's tornado of treasure.

"You look tired, little squirrel," the leontaur purred.

"Dead tired," Witch-Hazel answered, slinging the satchel over her shoulder. "And hungry," she added, noticing the hollow feeling in her belly she hadn't had time to notice before.

"I'd offer to share a meal with you." The leontaur grinned savagely. "But I don't think you'd like for me to eat a meal right now."

Witch-Hazel shivered, but she didn't have the energy left to be scared. Instead, she mechanically reached over her shoulder, groped around in the knapsack on her back, and pulled out a crocus bulb. That would do. She munched on it. The fleshy bulb tasted green and fresh. It gave her energy and filled her belly.

Between bites, Witch-Hazel asked, "Are you going to show me the way back out of this maze? Or do I have to pass another test first?"

"This time it's a riddle," the leontaur purred.

Witch-Hazel's tail drooped down and lay along the stone ground like a discarded rag. "I'm not good at riddles."

"Give this one a try before you give up." The leontaur rose from her crouch to stand on all four of her leonine legs, human arms crossed over her chest. "How far will a creature of treetops voyage under dirt and ground to find the lost Celestial Fragments?"

"As far as it takes for her to find them," Witch-Hazel answered in a rush. The words tripped over her tongue so fast that they were long gone, echoing in the giant cavern, before she realized that she'd been answering a riddle, and riddles have twists and tricks in them. It was too late to draw the words back.

But the leontaur's grin softened, replacing the malicious toothy edge with a gentle close-lipped fondness. "I'll take you to the abandoned mole village on the Eastern side of King Wendall's labyrinth. From there, you should be able to find your way deeper down."

Witch-Hazel enjoyed the ride on the leontaur's back, nestled once again between the tawny furred shoulders. The leontaur had an easy gait, but this time Witch-Hazel didn't let it rock her to sleep. She hoped to be back this way, possibly soon, with the Celestial Fragments in her pack. The leontaur would most likely be gone by then; Witch-Hazel would need to find her own way out.

Unfortunately, the twists and turns of the stone pathway the leontaur followed through the labyrinth soon dizzied Witch-Hazel into admitting to herself that she could never find her way out without help. Perhaps the abandoned mole village had passages leading both up and down. She had to hope. She didn't want to find the Celestial Fragments only to end up buried with them.

Of course, if she found all three Celestial Fragments, they would confer to her the strength, flight, and endless breath necessary to ascend to the All-Being's empire in the sky. A few miles of dirt between her and the sky couldn't stop her, right?

And yet Witch-Hazel worried, in spite of what she'd told the leontaur, she would give up. She would turn back without completing her quest.

8

THE LICHEN-COVERED CEILING of the cavern sloped downward, bringing the green glowing constellations closer as the leontaur approached the eastern edge of the cavern. At least according to the leontaur, it was the eastern edge. Witch-Hazel didn't know how to tell directions down here.

The ceiling had been much higher on the side of the cavern where Witch-Hazel had entered. She could see from her perch on the leontaur's back that the ceiling sloped upward toward the side where she'd entered, before turning sharply into a sheer stone wall taller than any tree she'd ever seen. On this side, the eastern side, the cavern shrunk to barely twice the leontaur's height before they reached the final stone wall.

While the ceiling had sloped downward, the bottom of the pits forming the labyrinth must have sloped upward, for they no longer plunged darkly down as though into a bottomless abyss. At first, the bottom of the pits had appeared like an illusion on either side of the path, a trick of the eye, but as the leontaur made her way to the edge of the cavern, the pits grew more and more shallow. By the time they reached the edge, the leontaur was hopping down into the pits and back up again to save time following the path's winding pattern.

"This is as far as I can take you," the leontaur said as they arrived at the stone wall. At this point, the pits and paths were no more than a decorative pattern carved into the floor.

A series of archways were set into the wall of the cavern, each of them mole-sized, meaning slightly cramped for a squirrel and barely big enough for a lion's paw. "Which one should I take?" Witch-Hazel asked, climbing down from the leontaur's back.

The leontaur shrugged her shoulders. "I've never been inside the mole village, so I can't tell you the way from here. All I can do is wish you luck, and give you this …" The leontaur brought her human hands together, steepling her slender fingers. Then she drew them apart, turning each hand as if she were drawing circles in the air. The tips of her fingers lit up, and the paths they traced shone. She drew circles, and then swirls, until the space between her hands burned brightly with pure white light.

Finally, the leontaur clapped her human hands together, extinguishing the shining lines of light. The clap echoed through the cavern, and when she opened her hands again, they held a glass vial with a bulbous end and a mouth stoppered by cork. It reminded Witch-Hazel of the glass bottle that had summoned Queen Amalah. Except this one was smaller, and instead of an opalescent liquid like trapped sunlight, this vial was filled with a red liquid. It looked like blood.

"Drink this if you find your strength waning, little adventurer," the leontaur said.

"What is it?" Witch-Hazel took the vial and tilted it in her paws. The red liquid coated the insides of the glass in a red film. Her stomach churned at the sight.

"A potion of strength," the leontaur purred. "Nothing more, nothing less." The leontaur began backing away, returning to the labyrinth. Before she turned her back on the squirrel, she said, "You will need it." Then she leapt into the air, spread her human arms wide as if they were wings and she was about to take flight. From the tips of her fingers, light spread out again. This time, it formed a bubble around her as she continued to rise into the air.

The bubble floated up and out toward the center of the cavern with the leontaur inside, arms spread wide and tufted tail swishing. In an instant, the bubble popped, flashing the cavern with momentary brightness.

When Witch-Hazel's eyes recovered, the leontaur was gone. She had winked out of sight like a memory slipping out of reach; once remembered, now forgotten. It both seemed impossible and like the only thing she could have possibly done. She had appeared from darkness; she disappeared into it too.

Witch-Hazel's pointy ears flattened, and she sighed deeply. *You cannot trust the darkness,* she thought. Yet she must continue to voyage through it.

Witch-Hazel stowed the potion of strength in her knapsack and drew one of the candle crystals from her satchel. She clacked the round rock hard against the stone floor, and then held its blue light up to the nearest archway. Examining the stone of the archway in the candle crystal's brighter light, she could make out carved lettering that curved over the top of the arch. The other archways had lettering over them as well.

At first, the shape of the letters was not familiar to her, but as Witch-Hazel examined the figures, she realized that she could make out words from them. The script was more slanted and angular than the writing she was used to, and the words were spelled strangely, but she could make sense of them.

The archway in front of her was labelled, "Tu Thy Uppur Warren." Beside it were archways labelled, "Tu Thy Mid-Livils," "Tu Thy Lowur Warren," and "Thy Mynes."

Witch-Hazel remembered the sonorous words of the snake's song, words that she had heard so long ago ... It felt like a lifetime of darkness and ghosts had passed since she stood in the sunlight, transfixed by the snake's song.

The Celestial Fragments wouldn't be in the mines. They had fallen from the heavens, not grown here in the darkness. Besides, the mines would have been picked over for those treasures on Wendell's dais long, long ago. Anything precious in the mines must have already been whisked away by Queen Amalah.

Witch-Hazel needed to find her way deeper under the earth, but the mines were not the way. She chose the archway labelled, "To Thy Lowur Warren."

Still hungry, Witch-Hazel pulled a tulip bulb from her knapsack and munched it as she marched down the ancient mole tunnels. After a long narrow passage, much like the dirt tunnels that had brought her to Wendell's maze in the first place, the tunnel opened up, wide enough for several squirrels to walk abreast, although Witch-Hazel could never imagine several squirrels down in these tunnels. She was having a hard enough time believing that she'd come all the way down here herself, and yet the evidence was all around: cold earth under her claws, dank dust in her nostrils, and echoes in her pointed ears unlike any sound in the swaying branches of a maple tree.

Her own footsteps echoed around the twists and turns of the tunnel, making it sound like someone else was approaching her, or sometimes leading the way. The light of the candle crystal cast her own squirrel-shaped shadow on the curved halls like a wraith of darkness. She tried not to think about Salal-Berry.

Witch-Hazel passed doors and branching tunnels with more of the mole-writing on them: "Hier Be Thy Markut," "Wilcum to Librury," and "Midicin Und Hielers." Witch-

Hazel looked into a few of the shops—there were stacks of empty baskets, abandoned rickety furniture, or other traces of what mole life had been like.

Witch-Hazel stopped at the library and flipped through a couple dusty, fragile tomes, but it was hard to read the tiny, angular text by the soft light of a candle crystal. She thought about bringing a few books with her, but books were heavy, and she likely had a long way to go.

The history of the moles would have to wait for a different adventurer to find their way down here.

Without the sun to mark time, Witch-Hazel had no idea how long she'd been traveling, always picking the path that sloped downward. When she felt her paws could carry her no farther, she checked the burrows she passed until she found one that seemed to have been a residence rather than a shop.

Witch-Hazel placed her knapsack, satchel, and fire-thorn swords on a wooden bureau in the small, rounded burrow and bedded down in an old empty nest made of twigs, straw, and bits of fur. She took her blue coat out of her knapsack and shrugged into it, hoping to ward off the chill that had been growing as she descended through this abandoned mole city.

Sleep didn't come easily, as she listened to her own breathing echo in the enclosed space of the burrow, wondering about the mole who'd built this home. So Witch-Hazel pulled the flask of her sister's pear cider out of her knapsack and drank herself to sleep, singing nut-gathering ballads to drown out the echoes until her tongue was too clumsy from cider to slur the words anymore.

Witch-Hazel slept soundly and woke suddenly. She'd been dreaming about the All-Being, a beautiful shifting image that fled the moment she opened her eyes, but she awoke to yet another ghost mole, this one screaming at her like wind roaring through branches and glaring with burning, red eyes from its shimmery, foggy form.

Witch-Hazel leapt from the nest, grabbed her fire-thorn swords and tried to discern a physical component of the ghost—like the honor guard's skulls—she could attack. But this ghost was nothing more than fog and noise. Its scream curdled the air and pierced Witch-Hazel's pointed ears, but when the ghost assaulted her, its bulky digging claws felt as insubstantial as a cold breeze.

Rattled but unharmed, Witch-Hazel gathered up her packs and left the ghost's home. She was still tired, but she'd get no more sleep in that haunted burrow.

Witch-Hazel's trek took her deeper into the lower warrens, and the burrows increased in density as she approached the center of the long abandoned village. Mole ghosts screamed at her as she passed their homes. Several ghost merchants attacked her as she passed their shops, but while their incorporeal claws felt like ice water running through her fur, they caused no real harm, only rattling her jangled nerves. Until she reached the town hall …

The passage opened up into a space large enough for a hundred moles to congregate. Stone pews faced towards one side of the wide room, and a granite statue of a mole covering its eyes with its forepaws towered over them.

Witch-Hazel stopped to stare at the statue and was taken off-guard when a mole ghost barreled toward her from between the pews, wielding a sword in a disembodied, skeletal paw. "Infidel!" the ghost screamed, slashing at her with the sword. The blade gleamed in the light of her candle crystal, for unlike her own firethorns, it was a true sword forged from metal. It bit into her chest, glancing off of her ribcage and tearing her coat. "None but moles may see the statue of the Blind God!"

Before the mole cleric could strike again, Witch-Hazel dropped her candle crystal and drew both of her firethorn swords. As she parried the cleric's metal blows, she wondered what had become of the rest of its skeleton to leave behind only the bones of a single forepaw.

Witch-Hazel's shadow danced eerily as she hopped back and forth, dueling the cleric above the discarded candle crystal. The cleric cast no shadow, except for its skeletal paw and sword.

With every blow, Witch-Hazel tried to force the sword and paw lower toward the ground. She was not practiced at swordplay and the cleric's sword sliced a notch in her left ear and left two bright lines of blood seeping through the fabric on her right shoulder before a lucky dodge allowed her to pin the metal sword against the back of one of the stone pews.

Witch-Hazel held the one firethorn sword firmly, keeping the cleric's weapon pinned while she dropped the other wooden weapon. She fumbled with her free paw on the ground until she felt the rocky curve of the candle crystal. She lifted the glowing stone and crashed it hard against the cleric's skeletal paw. She struck the cleric's paw again and again, repeatedly smashing the candle crystal into the bleached bones.

The ghost mole screamed in pain and then dissipated like fog in the morning as the skeletal hand fell to pieces. The shining sword clattered to the stone floor, but Witch-Hazel continued smashing the skeletal paw, causing the candle crystal to glow brighter and brighter, until nothing was left of the ghostly cleric but bone dust.

Finally, the candle crystal began to dim, even though Witch-Hazel continued to smash it against the crumbled bones. It was going out. In a panic, Witch-Hazel smashed the round stone harder and harder, now focused on trying to bring back its light. But its flecks of blue crystal dulled until all that was left was darkness and the feel of the rocky sphere in Witch-Hazel's paw.

She dropped the useless stone and stood in the darkness, chest heaving and ears still ringing from the sound of stone against stone. Her shoulder, ribs, and left ear stung where the cleric's sword had cut her. Her poor winter coat, though still warm, was tattered and stained.

Witch-Hazel dropped down to the floor and sat on her fluffy tail. She reached into her satchel, pulled out a fresh candle crystal and lit it with a single, sparing blow to the back of the stone pew beside her. She had only one more candle crystal left after this one. Then she would be plunged into eternal darkness, a squirrel buried alive.

By the dim blue light, Witch-Hazel searched her knapsack for the leaves of her namesake. When she found the witch-hazel leaves, she crushed one and rubbed it against her cuts, making them sting even more sharply. But they were less likely to become infected.

Gingerly, Witch-Hazel touched her ear and felt the shape of the missing notch. She'd be marked by this journey for life now. Silly squirrel had ventured underground where squirrels don't belong, and her perfect pointy ear would always be deformed because of it.

Witch-Hazel wished there were a lake or stream nearby where she could look at her reflection and see the damage. Then she noticed the gleam of the cleric's sword, discarded on the ground beside her. She lifted the sword and tilted the blade. It felt good in her paws. The hilt was comfortable and plain, made from a dark wood and simple silver for the pommel and guard. It was decorated only with runic etchings carved into the wood, but Witch-Hazel could not read them.

Witch-Hazel looked at herself in the sword's silver face. Her triangular ear was crusted with blood, but the missing notch made her look fierce. Especially given the gauntness in her gray-furred face and the haunted look in her previously sparkling black eyes.

Witch-Hazel no longer looked like the buffoon who would always come in last at acorn tag. She looked like a soldier from some long-forgotten war.

The lonely squirrel barked a hollow laugh at herself and remembered Salal-Berry laughing at her. She was going crazy down here. Any squirrel would.

But she had a quest. Three treasures to find and a god to meet.

Witch-Hazel tucked the metal sword carefully into her belt and left her firethorns behind. She had a better weapon now.

9

The screams of ghost moles no longer rattled Witch-Hazel as she strode through their abandoned city. She wondered what had happened to their city to leave so many of them in unrest in their afterlife, but she wasted no time on them, simply placing one paw in front of the other and traveling as quickly as she could, down, down through their tunnels.

The burrows thinned. She passed fewer shop entrances. The path branched less often, until eventually it was a single narrow tunnel with rough walls, twisting and turning haphazardly. It no longer felt like a structure that moles had carved and cared for, merely a single mole's reckless exploration into the deeps. And then not even that. The walls slanted until the one on the left merged with the floor, and the one on the right curved into the ceiling. Witch-Hazel felt she was no longer following a tunnel at all, only clambering downwards, slant-wise through a crack, a flaw in the earth.

She dug her claws in the dirt; if her paws slipped, she didn't know how far she would fall, sliding down into dirt and darkness. Then she heard voices, bubbling up from beneath her. She wondered what supernatural horror awaited her down below: More ghosts? Undead kings? Crazy queens? Another sphinx with tricks and riddles? In her distraction, Witch-Hazel lost her footing and tumbled in a scree of loose dry dirt down the steeply slanting crack in the earth. She lost hold of her candle crystal, and it rolled ahead of her. Her claws weren't strong enough to grab a purchase, so she pulled out her new sword and jammed it into the ground.

Witch-Hazel found herself hanging off the edge of a cliff, at least an old oak's height above the ground, clinging to her new sword. Her tail flipped about wildly, and her back paws kicked uselessly against the cliff side. Her heart raced, beating inside her chest like a drum foretelling the end of her quest: dashed against rocks, lost in the dark, failed at everything she'd ever attempted in life.

"Who goes there?" a voice called from below. It didn't sound supernatural. It sounded like a belly laugh. Resonant, amused, and jovial.

A second voice, much higher pitched but still amused, cried out, "I think that's a squirrel! Ho, up there! Are you a squirrel?"

The deeper voice rumbled, "What would a squirrel be doing *down here?*"

"A squirrel could ask the same about us," the higher voice said wryly.

Witch-Hazel twisted about, trying to turn her head far enough to see the creatures beneath her, but she couldn't do it without losing her grip on the hilt of her sword. She let out a squeal of exasperation. She'd have to hope the creatures were as unthreatening as they sounded. "I could use some help up here!"

"Hold on … Hold on …" the deep voice said. "Okay, let go!"

"Are you kidding?!" Witch-Hazel shrieked. Her paws were slipping, but she knew there was a long fall beneath her.

"Do I sound like I'm kidding?" The laughter in the deep voice *did* make it sound like it was kidding.

But Witch-Hazel had very few choices. She lost her hold and fell. For a moment, she was free. It was like when she would jump from one tree to the next. For a few seconds, she'd hang in the air, totally free from the chains of the Earth. A creature of the sky.

Then the moment ended, and the wind was knocked out of her. She bounced. When she landed again, it was softer. She was stretched out on her back, lying on some sort of fabric, stretched taut.

"Twiggy here built you a trampoline," the higher voice said. It was an otter. A very handsome river otter with a wide nose and a wider smile, wearing a dark green jerkin. He held out a paw to help Witch-Hazel up. "You can call me Fish-Breath. Twiggy does."

Witch-Hazel took the otter's paw and looked past him to see Twiggy—a chubby beaver with a bashful buck-toothed smile, wearing a surprisingly frilly ruffled sundress. Both the otter and the beaver were easily twice Witch-Hazel's height.

"All I did was attach the frame packs to each other and stretch one of the blankets between them," Twiggy said in her deep, jolly voice. "Anyone else would have done the same."

"I would not have," Fish-Breath insisted. "I'd have let the squirrel fall on her own tail. Now, can we get these packs separated again? I hope you haven't damaged my favorite blanket …"

"Every one of your belongings is your *favorite* one," Twiggy muttered, beginning to deconstruct the temporary trampoline.

"That's right," Fish-Breath agreed. "That's why they're my belongings. Why bother owning something that's not your favorite? Now, speaking of belongings," he gave Witch-Hazel a very serious, whiskers-downturned look. "Will you be wanting that sword back?" He pointed at the mole cleric's sword, far above, almost lost in the darkness but still sticking out of an opening in the cliff side.

Witch-Hazel sighed. "Yes, I would." She wished she'd thought to wrench it free before falling. On the other paw, then she'd have been falling with a big old metal sword in her paws. That would probably have been very dangerous. Possibly lethal.

"No problem," Fish-Breath said. "Twiggy? Can you rig something up for this situation?"

"Already on it," Twiggy answered. The two frame packs, built from wooden frames and muslin packs, were already separated, and she leaned them up against the cliff face before throwing the blanket that had been stretched between them at Fish-Breath.

The blanket hit the otter squarely in the face, and he said with a muffled voice from under the fabric, "Thanks!" He folded the blanket up and tucked it under one short arm. "Now, while Twiggy gets your sword, let's deal with the really important question: what kind of food do you have packed in those bags there?"

The otter eyed the squirrel's knapsack and satchel hungrily, and Witch-Hazel clutched them closer. She was glad that her sunflower pendant was already tucked out of sight inside her coat. His eager expression reminded her of Salal-Berry, and Witch-Hazel was struck with the image of both the otter and beaver melting down to rattling skeletons and fighting her for food their rib cages wouldn't even hold. She had no desire to battle skeletons who loomed over her, twice her size. At least the mole ghosts had been smaller than she was

Witch-Hazel backed away from the otter, but she backed right into the cliff side. Her paw stubbed on a rock, and she looked down to see the candle crystal she'd dropped. It was still glowing, but the light looked faint here. It wasn't the only light to see by. There was another light, warm and yellow, coming from a passage leading away from the cliff wall. She picked the candle crystal up and tucked it back inside her satchel.

"Hey now," Fish-Breath said, holding his paws out, palms open. "We're not going to steal your food, but the spicy root soup that I've whipped up is kind of thin. If you'll be wanting to share it with us, you might want to offer a few ingredients—something to zip it up, make it a little more hearty."

Witch-Hazel blinked. "Root soup?" That sounded good, and a few of her tulip bulbs might be perfect for it. But she'd been fighting ghosts and skeletons for nearly as long as she could remember, and she'd grown skeptical of anyone down here under the earth. Especially two river-folk who seemed painfully out of place. Although it might be a good sign that they seemed out of place. She was out of place too. "Can I see the soup?" she asked.

"It's over here," Fish-Breath gestured away from the cliff side, around a bend in the cavern. "Still simmering on the fire."

So that's where the light was coming from, Witch-Hazel realized. Now that she knew, she could see the warmth and flickering of the light on the cavern's dirt walls. It eased an ache, deep in her soul. There was a natural quality to the movement of the light, not unlike sunlight filtered through gently swaying leaves. It reminded her of home.

Suddenly Witch-Hazel felt light-headed. On unsteady paws, she followed the flickering light. As she rounded the bend in the cliff side, her eyes were overwhelmed by the orange and yellow glow of fire light. She knelt down before the campfire on the dirt ground, curled her tail around herself like a blanket and began to comb the long, gray fur with her claws. The ground was cold under her, but the heat from the fire kissed her nose and warmed the fur on her tail.

The otter swaggered past her, leaned over the fire, and tended a tarnished copper pot hanging just above the licking flames. He stirred the pot with a long wooden spoon, and a wholesome smell of roots and spices wafted over to Witch-Hazel. The scent made her nose twitch eagerly in spite of her reservations.

"Do you promise you're not a ghost?" Witch-Hazel asked.

"Cross my heart and hope to die," Fish-Breath said, crossing his heart with the wooden spoon. "Although I suppose if I die, then I might become a ghost. Better to hope for something else ..." He trailed off, chewing the whiskers on one side of his muzzle while he thought. "I know! Cross my heart and hope for rain!"

"For rain?" Witch-Hazel asked, bewildered. "What?"

"Well, it's not going to rain down here," Fish-Breath explained. "But I sure do wish it would!" He wiggled his long back, shaking his rudder-tail from side to side. "I could use a few drip-drops on this dry pelt, but all we've got down here is dust and dirt and rocks!"

"And ancient swords," Twiggy said with a slight whistle between her teeth. The beaver held the mole cleric's sword out, hilt-first to the huddling, preening squirrel.

"Thank you," Witch-Hazel said, taking the sword with one paw. She felt safer already. "How did you get it down?"

"A simple grappling hook," the beaver answered over her shoulder as she headed back for the frame packs around the bend.

Twiggy carried one pack and then the other over to the fireside; then she settled down near Witch-Hazel. She sat on her broad, flat tail and leaned her back against one of the packs. It looked comfortable, but Witch-Hazel didn't think her satchel or knapsack would work the same way. They weren't big enough.

"Give us some soup, Fish-Breath," Twiggy said. She reached into the frame pack beside her and held out a wooden bowl toward the otter. Fish-Breath took Twiggy's bowl. Then he pulled another out of his own frame pack.

Witch-Hazel hadn't brought a bowl. She didn't suppose that Twiggy and Fish-Breath had brought an extra, but before she could ask—

"You can borrow mine," the otter said, beginning to ladle the thin but fragrant soup into his bowl. "I'll eat after you're finished."

"Wait," Witch-Hazel said, shamed by the otter's generosity. She took her knapsack off and pulled out three tulip bulbs. Their dry, papery skin crinkled in her paws, but the beginnings of green shoots poking out of their ends bespoke how ready they were to be eaten. "Cook these into the soup first."

Fish-Breath's answering grin was brighter than the campfire. He poured the soup he'd ladled into the bowl back into the pot. The glassy broth splashed and sizzled. Then he put the bowl down and reached out to take the tulip bulbs from Witch-Hazel.

Fish-Breath hefted the three bulbs in his paws, testing their weight, and then he threw them, one at a time, into the air. The yellow-brown bulbs danced between his paws, jumping through the air in a cheerful circle as the otter juggled them.

"He's going to keep doing that until you either laugh or applaud," Twiggy said.

Fish-Breath kept throwing the bulbs higher and higher, a comically horrified expression painted onto his muzzle, as though he really didn't know if he could catch them. Suddenly, one of the bulbs flew right over his head, but it landed in a paw behind his back. It was as if the bulb were afraid to hit the ground and preferred Fish-Breath's webbed paw.

Witch-Hazel laughed and applauded. Fish-Breath bowed his head while the tulip bulbs dropped into the copper pot one at a time—plop, plop, plop!

"Thank goodness," Twiggy said. "Maybe this means we'll eventually get to eat."

Fish-Breath stirred the bulbs around the pot several times and then set the wooden spoon aside. "While those are cooking," he said. "Why don't you tell us how a tree-surfer like you ended up in an underground labyrinth like this?"

"A quest," Witch-Hazel said dully, her voice sounding haunted and her thoughts miles away, up above the ground. Her paw strayed from brushing her tail to touch the sunflower pendant hanging around her neck. The feel of the inset topaz's angular facets reminded her of its cheerful, sunny color. It felt like an emblem of home.

"We're on a quest too," the beaver said proudly, whistling through her buck teeth in excitement. "We're going to unblock the ancient aqueducts of the underground and restore the ancestral accomplishments of my people!"

"That's right!" Fish-Breath agreed with a grin. "This whole dusty dried-up husk of a labyrinth will be filled with joyous slippy-slidey gushes of water when we're done. So much water, it'll flow against the grain of the earth and open up the highway to the sky."

"*The river that flows in endless looping circles* ..." Witch-Hazel muttered, remembering the words of the snake's song.

The otter and beaver grew very quiet. The way they looked at Witch-Hazel made her uncomfortable.

"It's from a song I heard ... somewhere," Witch-Hazel said, pulling her tail up under her chin, wishing she could hide under it entirely but knowing that would look weird.

"It's from *The Song of the All-Being,*" Twiggy said reverently. Her buck teeth didn't whistle this time. "Every year, all the animals of the rivers and lakes, all the water peoples, come together for the Joining of Many Waters Ceremony. One of the high priests sings *The Song of the All-Being.* Usually a turtle. Sometimes a frog. I don't know where a squirrel would have heard it."

"I heard it from a snake," Witch-Hazel breathed, afraid she was revealing too much. She knew her people, the squirrels, didn't trust snakes. She didn't know how beavers and otters felt about snakes, but these were much larger mammals than her. Perhaps they were less afraid of serpents. Or perhaps she was signing her death warrant by admitting to larger mammals that she was on a snake's errand, doing a snake's bidding. They could take her supplies and leave her to starve in the darkness.

Witch-Hazel might have fought off dozens of ghost moles, but she didn't like her odds against two mammals twice her size and warm with beating hearts. Nonetheless, she had begun telling the truth. It was too late to stop. With her squirrel-heart racing, Witch-Hazel said, "The snake sent me on this quest—to gather the missing Celestial Fragments and restore contact with the All-Being."

Neither otter nor beaver spoke. Fish-Breath picked up the wooden spoon and stirred the soup again. "It's ready," he said, grabbing one of the wooden bowls. He ladled steaming broth into the bowl until it was nearly full. Finally he scooped up a single tulip bulb and plopped it in.

Fish-Breath held the bowl out to Witch-Hazel. Cautiously, she took it, reluctant to seem too eager. She mustn't show her fear and uncertainty.

Fish-Breath filled the second bowl, again apportioning exactly one bulb into it, and handed it to Twiggy. Then he set the stirring spoon down and chewed on his whiskers.

The wooden bowl felt pleasantly warm in Witch-Hazel's paws, and the savory scent of the steam made her stomach cramp with desire. Yet she felt too vulnerable to eat. Like she needed to be ready to drop the bowl, reach for her sword, and fight at any moment.

Twiggy took a sip of her soup, tilting the bowl to drink from it. After her sip, she said, "Was it a water snake who sang you the song?"

"I … don't know different kinds of snakes …" Witch-Hazel stuttered. "It had yellow eyes." That was all she could remember. Those mesmerizing yellow eyes.

The beaver snorted, but she didn't say anything. Instead, she took another long drink of her soup.

Fish-Breath stopped chewing his whiskers and said, "It doesn't matter where you got your quest." He stared levelly at Twiggy, and the beaver didn't challenge him. "It's the same quest as ours, simply using different methods." Fish-Breath turned to Witch-Hazel and added, "We should work together. Who knows, maybe we'll find those pesky Celestial Fragments clogging up the source of the never-ending river's waters." He winked at the little squirrel, and she felt her stomach unknot. "With a merry band like ours, we can hardly fail. One way or another, I plan to dance a waltz with the All-Being when our quests are done." Fish-Breath shimmied his shoulders as if to a jaunty beat.

Twiggy slurped the last of her broth and plucked her boiled tulip bulb out of her bowl with a surprisingly delicate paw. Her forepaws weren't webbed like her back paws, or like all four of Fish-Breath's. The two aquatic mammals must have very different styles of swimming.

"I'd like to see that waltz," Twiggy said, handing Fish-Breath the now-empty bowl.

The otter fixed himself a bowl of soup, and Twiggy nibbled on the softened tulip bulb she'd plucked from hers. "This is good!" the beaver exclaimed. "Thank you, squirrel."

"Witch-Hazel," she said. "My name is Witch-Hazel."

"That's a lovely name." Fish-Breath's muzzle split into a wide smile that Witch-Hazel could picture herself getting used to. "Now, let me tell you a story, Witch-Hazel ..."

The otter launched into a tall tale, alternating snippets of story with sips of his soup, telling about the time his mother had stretched a river up over a witch-hazel tree, an oak tree, and a towering silver maple to build a longer waterslide for him and his litter mates. Fish-Breath told the story with a perfect mix of outrageous jocularity and wide-eyed, self-effacing faux-naivety. Even Twiggy, who had clearly heard many of this otter's stories before, couldn't help giggling.

As Witch-Hazel listened, she relaxed, and hunger overtook her. She felt safe enough to eat now. She lifted the warm wooden bowl to her muzzle and sipped the savory broth, the flavors of many different roots and spices mingling together. It tasted like companionship.

10

After dinner and story-telling, the trio slept around the embers of their campfire. Witch-Hazel's rest was interrupted only by the soft whistling-snores of Twiggy and Fish-Breath's quiet dream mutters about waterfalls and white water rafting. These sounds were much more peaceful, much more welcome than the unsettling screams of undead moles.

Witch-Hazel slept soundly, and she awoke feeling more rested than she had since before she'd first heard the snake's song. She felt ready to face whatever challenges these caverns could throw at her.

Fish-Breath served the remaining root soup cold for breakfast, and once they were all packed up, Witch-Hazel handed out buttery-soft black walnuts to munch as they hiked down into the darkness.

Witch-Hazel continued carrying one of her candle crystals to light the way, but now its dim glimmer of blue light was complemented by a mechanical torch of Twiggy's. The beaver claimed to have constructed her torch from rare bits of metal she'd found and pieces of glass she'd purchased from another beaver who'd made the transparent stuff by melting sand in a furnace. Twiggy told Witch-Hazel about technological wonders the little squirrel had never imagined before—river turbines powering torches to light the city of Riverton all night long; mechanical boxes that stayed ice cold even in the heat of summer; and ceramic disks with grooves on them that could preserve and play back a voice over and over again.

Witch-Hazel had no idea there were cities like Riverton, where both Twiggy and Fish-Breath came from. If she had heard a song about Riverton before beginning this journey, instead of the snake's song, she would have gone there instead of voyaging down into these dark depths. She said as much, and once again, the beaver and otter grew really quiet in response to her words. It made her nervous.

The three travelers marched on through the eerily lit cavern, their shadows dancing along on the jagged walls. The dirt ground absorbed the sound of their footsteps. Without Twiggy telling stories of Riverton and its technology, the silence was stifling.

"When we've restored the never-ending river," Fish-Breath said, "you should come home to Riverton with us. We'd love to show you around." He elbowed Twiggy with a short arm, and the beaver made a non-committal whistling sound.

After a few more steps, Twiggy held her mechanical torch forward and said, "Look, up ahead!" There were circles of silver, gleaming dully in the dark. Three of them, each one the size of Twiggy's broad flat tail.

Witch-Hazel rushed ahead, bushy tail twitching eagerly. "I've seen a puzzle like this before," she said, eager to show her new companions her worth. She put her paws up to the silver circles—they were medallions inset in a wooden door, like the golden ones that had guarded the original entrance to this underground dungeon. Each silver medallion had little figures etched into it. Instead of animals though, these figures were mostly trees, flowers, and tiny landscapes.

The top medallion was ringed entirely by pictures of different types of flowers; the bottom left medallion entirely with trees. But the pictures around the edges of the bottom right medallion were a variety of tiny scenes—a sunrise; a mountain range; a tree leaning over a lake; a castle with turrets and towers; a waterfall. Witch-Hazel wasn't sure what to make of these pictures. They all seemed out of place deep underground.

Then she touched a paw to the topaz sunflower pendant, resting against her fur, under her coat. It was out of place down here too.

The image of the sunflower on the upper silver medallion was strikingly similar. It could be a coincidence. But, maybe not. Everything in these tunnels felt filled with portent. Witch-Hazel reached toward the silver medallion, planning to turn it until the image of the sunflower was at the top.

Instead, the beaver shoved Witch-Hazel aside. "I've got this," she said. She turned her head until her tiny ear was right up against the stone door, between the silver medallions. She began turning the bottom left medallion, slowly, methodically.

"She's listening for clicks," Fish-Breath whispered, leaning in close to Witch-Hazel. "These puzzles are nothing more than mechanisms, and Twiggy's a wizard with mechanisms. It's basically like cracking a safe. She'd be an excellent bank-robber!"

The beaver shushed their whispers with a whistling, "Hush!" and continued turning the medallions.

Witch-Hazel couldn't hear any clicks, but then her ear wasn't pressed against the door. Twiggy made an excited chittering sound each time that she, apparently, heard one. When the third medallion finally clicked into place, Witch-Hazel noticed with a thrill of excitement that the sunflower image was indeed at the top. Though, neither of the images at the top of the other two medallions meant anything to her: a magnolia tree, rich with tulip-like blossoms, and the castle with turrets and towers, straight out of a fairy tale. With all the alternative images, Witch-Hazel might never have solved this puzzle on her own.

Twiggy shoved the heavy wooden door open.

As the squirrel followed her companions through the doorway, she slipped her paw under her coat and grasped the cool metal pendant hidden against her chest. She wanted to pull it out and look at it closely, but she also wanted to keep it secret. She wasn't sure how much significance it held. Suddenly, it seemed like it was a whole lot more than she'd realized.

On the other side of the wooden door, the cramped, craggy passage they'd been wandering opened up into a giant cavern. Unlike the cavern with the mole king's labyrinth, the floor of this one angled downward. The ground here was a slanting mountainside, laced with trickling rivulets and dripping creeks, winding their way down the slick and rocky slope. The slender fingers of water shone in a soft white light, emanating from deeper underground. Witch-Hazel couldn't make out the light's source from the stone doorway, set into the side of this underground mountain, but it was bright enough that she slipped her candle crystal back into its satchel.

"Water!" Fish-Breath cried. The otter shrugged out of his frame pack, threw the heavy bundle to the ground beside the wooden door, and sprinted on four feet toward the nearest rivulet. Once there, he rolled and somersaulted in the trickling water, soaking his green jerkin and thick fur. "We're getting close! I can feel it!" He giggled. Sparkling droplets of water clung to his whiskers and beaded all over the fur of his face.

Twiggy's muzzle split in a wide buck-toothed grin. She shrugged out of her frame pack, leaving it on the ground in the stone doorway as well, and chased after Fish-Breath. The beaver was less lithe and light on her feet than the otter, but she moved with hustle. When she got to the rivulet, she slapped her flat tail against the water, splashing the otter. He squeaked in delight.

The ensuing water fight was epic. The two aquatic mammals had most likely been separated from their native habitat for weeks underground. They splashed and wrestled, tumbling through the shallow water, bubbling over with joy at the simple sensation of wetness in their pelts.

More though, this was a sign that Twiggy and Fish-Breath were on the right path for their quest—they'd found the water, flowing down the side of this underground mountain. Now all they had to do was follow it.

Witch-Hazel's path was less clear. She stood in the stone doorway, watching the water mammals play, and wondering whether their path was the right path for her. The silver medallions felt like a sign—the last medallion puzzle had been a message from the snake who'd started her on this quest. And—she remembered with a leap of her heart—there had been a letter and gift waiting for her on the other side.

Witch-Hazel looked down at her hind paws, but there was nothing on the ground but loose stones and her companions' frame packs. She wrestled with the giant, heavy packs until she'd pushed their wood-and-muslin bulks aside enough to be sure there wasn't a note hidden under either of them. The squirrel was disappointed, but she wasn't ready to give up yet.

Witch-Hazel examined the stone doorway—it was a simple, blocky archway built into the mountainside. She clawed at the seams in the stone, but none of them had anything hidden in their creases. Witch-Hazel couldn't reach the flat top of the doorway, even on her tippy toes. The mountainside was especially steep around the doorway, so she hiked a ways out, hopping over rivulets, until she was at a gentler slope. She clambered up the mountainside until she was higher than the top of the stone doorway and then edged her way back over, careful not to lose her footing on the steeper stone. Even so, her claws screeched and slipped on the rock. By moving slowly, she managed to get over to the flat top of the doorway.

Sure enough, there was a piece of parchment, folded many times, held in place by a pile of dried up mushrooms with a candle crystal nestled on top. Witch-Hazel pulled the parchment carefully out from under the nest of mushrooms. When she unfolded it, the paper was stained but still readable:

"Clever-Brave Squirrel has made it far! Must be hungry—I have gathered Mushrooms. Clever-Brave Squirrel is close now. Do not lose sight. Wishes for Swift Paws, A Snake who Eagerly Awaits."

Witch-Hazel's tail flipped and quivered behind her, expressing the complicated feelings that the note inspired—excitement at the idea she was close; skepticism as to whether the snake, who'd failed at this quest itself, really knew if she was close; and trepidation at the idea of a snake eagerly awaiting.

Awaiting what?

Witch-Hazel had never promised to bring the Celestial Fragments to the snake if she found them. Perhaps the snake was planning to steal them.

Witch-Hazel slipped the note and the fresh candle crystal into her satchel. She picked up one of the mushrooms, touching it only with her claw tips and sniffed it, nose twitching. It smelled musty, earthy, but not bad. She took a nibble. The taste was strong and meaty. Witch-Hazel liked it. The flavor reminded her of year-old chestnut troves, forgotten under the dirt and found again after the nuts were all shrunken and wrinkly.

She gathered the dried mushrooms up in her paws and stuffed them into her knapsack with the remaining rations that she'd packed for herself. Then she hopped down from the top of the doorframe and began exploring this underground mountainside—if the snake had gathered the mushrooms here, she might be able to find some fresh ones.

The dried mushrooms were wrinkly and brown, but when Witch-Hazel found fresh mushrooms growing out of nooks and crannies in the mountainside, they were soft and pinky-gray. Their flavor was much subtler, more understated than in the dried ones. Witch-Hazel actually preferred the meaty flavor of the dried mushrooms, and she liked their chewy feel between her teeth. The fresh ones were bland, but she stuffed them in her knapsack too. They would dry.

"You don't want to get that bushy tail wet?" Fish-Breath called out, bounding across the mountainside toward her.

"I'm gathering mushrooms," Witch-Hazel explained. She held one of the fleshy fungi out for the otter.

Fish-Breath took the mushroom in his paw, sniffed it, eyed it skeptically, shook it by his ear as if listening to it, and then popped it in his muzzle. "Not bad. I can put these in our next soup."

Witch-Hazel approved of that plan. Fish-Breath was clearly a skilled cook—she wondered what kind of delicacies he could make if he weren't restricted to a campfire, a single copper pot, and scavenged ingredients. Maybe he'd cook for her when she visited Riverton after their quests were over.

The otter and beaver gathered up their frame packs, and the little crew hiked down the slippery mountainside. Every now and again, Fish-Breath cried, "Water slide!" and dropped to his belly in one of the streams to plummet down the mountainside headfirst in the icy water.

Twiggy stayed behind to walk with Witch-Hazel. The beaver was an aquatic mammal, but she was less aerodynamic than the otter. Also less reckless.

The three of them hiked all day—at least, it felt like all day. The hours stretched out endlessly, unmarked in this underground realm. The white glow in the distance never changed, growing neither brighter nor dimmer. It felt like they were trapped in a twilight purgatory, every paw step bringing them closer to a goal that receded farther into the distance.

Finally, Twiggy declared it was time to camp. They found a relatively flat stretch of the mountainside and pretended it was evening. Twiggy made a fire, and Fish-Breath cooked a mushroom soup. Witch-Hazel told them stories about her sisters and brothers back above the ground. Stories of trees and nuts, squabbling over treasure that was nothing more than a snack, and playing chase among the leaves.

Witch-Hazel missed her home.

11

Witch-Hazel awoke regularly throughout the night, startled out of her sleep by nightmares. She dreamed the rivulets and streams had tied themselves around her, wrapping her up in wet strands; then she dreamed they came gushing down, raining from the ceiling, filling up the cavern until their little camp floated away. Every dream ended with her gasping awake, convinced she was drowning.

She wished morning would come. She longed for pink and gold fingers of sunrise on the horizon, sunlight filtering through leaves. Instead, she half woke to see the stale light of the underground gloaming; always the same.

Finally, Witch-Hazel was woken from groggy sleep by Twiggy waving a bowl of cold mushroom soup under her nose.

"Eat up," the beaver said. "It's time to get cracking."

The three companions hiked down the hillside in silence. Fish-Breath hopped cheerfully from one stream to the next, always keeping his webbed hind paws wet. Witch-Hazel tried to keep her paws dry, but in the twilight darkness it was easy to miss shallow rivulets and end up slipping and skittering over wet rock.

Witch-Hazel wasn't sure, but it seemed like their breaks for meals stretched further and further apart. Eventually, they were no longer hiking, merely trudging. Ever downward. In tired, awkward silence. Even Fish-Breath didn't have the heart to dance with the rivulets any more. The only sign they were progressing at all was that the rivulets had widened from tiny trickles to small streams.

By the time they stopped to sleep again, Witch-Hazel was convinced several days had passed. Strange visions flitted past her eyes—the dark rock seemed to beat with her heart, breathing and sighing beneath her paws as if alive. Rocks stood up and followed them; other rocks circled them. She heard the snake's song whispering with the babble of the rivulets. She saw dark squirrels hidden in shadows and snake eyes laughing at her in the glint of light on water, but only from the corner of her eye. The visions flitted out of sight when she turned to see them better. She was hallucinating from exhaustion.

Twiggy dug up roots from between the rocks and started a fire. Fish-Breath cooked up a tulip bulb and mushroom soup, but Witch-Hazel was sound asleep before it was ready.

She awoke confused, hours later. She knew it was hours later, because the campfire was nothing more than smoldering embers. Her otter and beaver companions were sound asleep in their sleeping bags. Witch-Hazel only had her winter coat as a blanket and her lumpy knapsack as a pillow. So she was stiff and sore, but wide awake. She had slept soundly and long.

That's why she was confused when her dreams assaulted her. Waking nightmares filled her vision, but her brain was no longer addled from lack of sleep. Her eyes were clear and rested; yet she saw rocks rise and walk and circle the camp. Demonic snake eyes stared at her from all around, reflecting the pale light.

Witch-Hazel froze, every muscle unmoving. She watched the rocks and the eyes circling the camp until her own eyes started to make sense of them. Each moving rock had a flat top, and each pair of eyes rose above one of the flat rocks on short stalks. There were a dozen or so of these rocks with eyes.

"Crabs," Fish-Breath barked, sitting up in his sleeping bag.

As the otter spoke, the rocks broke apart, pieces of them rising upward like arms held to a darkened sky.

"Sharp pincers, too," the otter muttered, rubbing the sleep from his eyes.

The rock-like crabs clacked their pincers, and rivulets that had been running down the mountainside rose from the ground; water streamed through the air like ribbons, braiding around the camp.

"Sorcerous crabs." Fish-Breath shook his head. "I thought they were legends."

Twiggy shifted in her sleeping bag. "We're closer to the source than I'd realized. No more rest from here on."

Witch-Hazel had never heard legends of sorcerer crabs, but then she'd never heard of the endless river until the snake sang to her. Apparently, it hadn't sung enough. She was not prepared. But she picked up her sword stolen from the mole cleric, and its heft in her paw reassured her. These crabs looked solid—they could be hit by forged metal.

"What are you doing?" Twiggy asked. Both the beaver and otter were staring at the sword in the squirrel's paw.

"Preparing for battle?" Witch-Hazel said uncertainly. "Against the sorcerer crabs?" Neither of her companions had drawn weapons. In fact, Witch-Hazel realized that she didn't know if they even had weapons. Had they made it this far under the earth without being attacked by any mad squirrels or ghost moles? "Why don't either of you seem scared?"

"According to the legends," Twiggy said, "the crabs are the keepers of the endless river. They protect what we've come to fix. Why would we be scared?"

Witch-Hazel wasn't convinced, but Twiggy sounded certain of herself. Perhaps the demon-eyed crabs weren't hostile, merely disconcerting.

Witch-Hazel began to lower her sword. Then a ribbon of water whipped her in the face. She raised her sword, but it was not a shield against water whips. The ribbons of water cut right through her sword and stung as they lashed her shoulders and back. With a gurgle, Witch-Hazel tried to call out, but ended up with a mouthful of water. She wanted to whirl into battle, hacking her sword every which way, like a tiny gray-furred tornado. But she could scarcely see from water dripping in her eyes, and she couldn't risk harming her companions.

Witch-Hazel dropped the sword, and held her arms over her face, shielding her eyes from the water. She blinked until she could see again.

The circle of crabs had tightened around the camp, waving their pincers in the air, directing the assault of whipping rivulets like conductors of a watery orchestra.

Reminded of those sharp pincers, Witch-Hazel swore to herself and groped for her sword on the ground. Instead, she found her soggy knapsack and satchel shoved into her paws by Twiggy.

"Forget the sword," Twiggy said. "The crabs' bodies are living suits of armor. If they want to fight us, we need to take what we can and run." The beaver and otter had been scrambling to pack up as much of the camp as they could. Being hit in the face with ribbons of water didn't faze them like it did a squirrel.

"Even suits of armor have cracks in them," Witch-Hazel sputtered through another blast of water. Besides, who knew what would attack her next down here? She was not leaving behind her weapon.

Still Witch-Hazel halfway followed the beaver's instruction—she slung her satchel over her shoulder and her knapsack over her back before picking up the sword.

Then Witch-Hazel braced her hind paws, centered herself, and pointed the sword at the nearest crab. Its back was flat and gray like a rock, but the edge of its shell was lined with yellow-speckled spikes, and it swayed on skittery, segmented, insectile legs. Its pincers, held aloft, clacked like castanets, and its eyes glowed like tiny moons.

Witch-Hazel aimed for the eye-stalks and swung her sword. It was only after the sharpened shaft of metal was flying through the air that Witch-Hazel wondered whether the slice of a sword was a disproportional response to a few splashes of water. Sure, the water whips stung, but her body wasn't permanently damaged. Bruised, sure. But otherwise, when she dried off, she'd be fine.

The sword sliced through the eyestalks, and two tiny moons flew off into the darkness of the cavern. Leaving behind a crab without eyes. A sightless sorcerer. Several of the water whips flying through the air stopped still, hovered in place, and then rained down on the camp. The blind crab's pincers clacked and waved as if it were looking for its missing eyes.

Witch-Hazel heard a scream, but crabs can't scream. They don't have voices. It was her own voice, ripped from her throat by the horror of what she'd done. Yet only moments later, she swung the sword again—two of the crabs were rushing toward her, pincers clacking. She aimed at their eye stalks. What else could she do?

Water blasted the squirrel in her chest, knocking her out of balance, and her sword bounced harmlessly off one of the crab's backs. Witch-Hazel was almost relieved, until the other crab grabbed her sword's blade with its powerful pincer. She yanked at the sword's hilt, but her blade wouldn't break free from the crab's hold. Instead, she pulled the crab closer, legs scuttling over the slippery ground. The vice-like pincer, inches from her face, had a jagged edge.

Witch-Hazel's breath caught in her throat as the crab's other pincer reached for her. Before the jagged vice could clamp down on her leg, a pair of fuzzy arms grabbed her around the waist, tugging her backward. Witch-Hazel lost hold of her sword. The metal blade snapped in two with a musical twang under the pressure of the crab's claw. The other jagged pincer grazed her leg, cutting like a serrated knife, but it didn't have a chance to clamp down.

Without her sword, Witch-Hazel was unarmed and surrounded by living suits of armor wielding arms like giant saw-toothed scissors. Before the horror of her situation could fully sink in, Fish-Breath, whose arms were still wrapped around her, threw her onto a sled improvised from his frame pack. He jumped on after her, and the momentum of his body shoved the sled into motion. It caught the flow of a rivulet, bowled right between two of the crabs, and whooshed away from the camp.

Twiggy followed closely behind on the other frame pack. The two sleds sped down the mountainside, bumping and bouncing along the babbling rivulet. The circle of crabs and their magically manipulated tendrils of water receded into the distance behind them, cloaked in darkness.

But the image of the blinded crab continued to burn brightly in Witch-Hazel's imagination.

12

THROUGH BLEARY EYES, vision blurred by tears and water dripping from her soggy ears, Witch-Hazel saw the light break on the horizon. The pale glow they'd been chasing resolved into torchlight flickering in the windows of a castle across an underground lake. All the rivulets, including the one she was rafting down with Fish-Breath, fed into the lake.

The rivulets joined together, combining into fewer but wider rivers as they neared the lake. Fortunately, the improvised sled made from the frame pack proved sea worthy. It floated along the deepening waterway, and the bumpy ride smoothed out as the babbling brook settled down into a murmuring river.

Up ahead, the castle's torch-lit windows reflected on the lake's wine-dark surface. Its turrets looked like a row of square-edged teeth; the tallest towers on either end jutted up like the sharp points of fangs. The underground castle leered at Witch-Hazel from across the lake, a terrifying smile ready to swallow her whole.

Fish-Breath wrapped his arms around Witch-Hazel again and gave her a squeeze. His whiskers tickled her pointed ear as he whispered, "See the castle? We're almost there!"

Witch-Hazel poked at the frame pack under her. It was floating for now, but the muslin cloth wasn't water proof. As water seeped inside, the pack floated lower, slowly sinking. "We can't ride these all the way across that lake."

Fish-Breath stuck his long thick tail into the river behind them and steered his tail like a rudder. The frame pack drifted ashore and ran aground. Twiggy came up behind them on her own frame pack, using her broad flat tail like a paddle.

"Do you think you can make a boat for us to cross the lake in?" Fish-Breath asked. "We could swim but—" He looked at Witch-Hazel.

Twiggy didn't answer. The beaver was too busy already, pawing through the water-logged frame packs. She spread out their supplies on the wet ground and examined the material she had to work with.

Witch-Hazel looked at the contents of the frame packs as Twiggy laid them out. She wasn't looking for materials to build a boat. She was hoping to find weapons, but all they had were sleeping bags, bowls, spoons, sundry small devices like the mechanical torch, soggy rations, and a copper pot.

The copper pot would make an awkward weapon, but it was the closest they had.

Witch-Hazel missed her stolen sword, and even her discarded firethorns, fiercely. All she had left of her own was the satchel of candle crystals and knapsack of rations, now very soggy.

"Why did they attack us?" Witch-Hazel asked, lifting the copper pot, feeling its heft. "We hadn't done anything."

"Maybe they've gone crazy down here in the dark," Fish-Breath mused. "Protecting a broken turbine; worshipping a defunct engine; practicing their arts in waters run stale."

Witch-Hazel put the copper pot down and stared at Fish-Breath. His eyes had gone all dreamy; his whiskers quivered. "You weren't expecting a fight. You were expecting to be welcomed."

"Once upon a time, this castle—" He gestured across the lake at the Halloween building, "—was the capital of the aquatic world. Otters made pilgrimages here, and yes, they were welcomed with feasts and celebration and the most beautiful services worshipping the All-Being. I knew it wouldn't be like that …"

His tone said otherwise. He had expected it to be exactly like that.

Twiggy slammed the frame pack she was holding down on the slippery rock ground. "There's a difference between decrepit and perverted. We expected the machines to be broken down, abandoned, or perhaps decayed beyond the sorcerer crabs' skills to repair." Her buck teeth whistled. "They are magicians, not mechanics after all. Yet the Order of Decapodia Crustacea is blessed by the All-Being! Their line descends from the very first crustacean, constructed from pieces of the All-Being's own shed shell! If they can go mad …"

"What hope is there for the world," Fish-Breath finished her thought.

"Forget the world." Witch-Hazel hefted the copper pot again and imagined slamming it into a sacred decapod's shell. She could hear scuttling claws in the distance. The crabs were following them. She took a step toward the lake's edge and nearly stumbled to the ground. Her leg seared with pain. Wet blood soaked her fur in a ragged line where the crab's claw had cut her.

She did not want to die down here.

"But the turbines …" Fish-Breath gestured with a webbed paw at the castle; the building glared back at them with its jagged rictus. "Twiggy can fix them."

"Not if she's dead." Witch-Hazel had come down here chasing a shiny stash, glory, and redemption for her clumsy, forgetful, incompetent self. She had wanted to meet the All-Being, but she didn't want to meet the All-Being enough to do it dead. That was not the path she wanted to walk. And maybe she still wasn't good at finding hidden treasure; maybe she was still terrible at being a squirrel; maybe she couldn't help Twiggy and Fish-Breath save the world … But she could save them. She could be good at being a friend. Maybe even a leader.

The crab claws kept clacking. The itchy sound of it grew closer. Worse, ripples appeared on the surface of the lake, dozens of them, traveling in lines toward Witch-Hazel and her friends. Crab sorcerers were coming from every direction.

Witch-Hazel wished for a tree to climb: a strong trunk to scurry up like a ladder and broad branches to hide in, safely above the clacking claws.

There was no tree. There was no shortcut out of here, back to the world of sky and grass and fields of flowers. Witch-Hazel touched her paw to the sunflower pendant tucked inside her coat, felt the angles of its topaz with her claw tips, and then clutched it tight. She whispered, too quiet for her companions to hear, almost too loud for praying to a god, "Give me strength. Give me cleverness. Show me a way out of here."

From above, the glowing double moons of crab eyes appeared in the darkness; from below, exoskeletal bodies broke the surface of the lake. They were surrounded by mecha-like sorcerers. Ribbons of water rose into the air, snaking toward the small band of mammals.

The sunflower pendant vibrated in Witch-Hazel's paws. At first, she wasn't sure if she was imagining it. Then she felt the vibration humming in her bones. The hum grew louder, stronger, stretched out to fill the cavern. It shook the ribbons of water snaking toward them; the ribbons wobbled and finally broke into pieces, raining down harmlessly without the force of the crabs' magic behind them. The crabs themselves wobbled on their claws—tripping, falling, smacking into the ground.

And still the humming grew. Witch-Hazel felt all her fur fluff up, stand on end, shaken by the hum and prickled by her fear. The crabs' exoskeletons began to crack as the vibration of the hum resonated with their suddenly brittle shells.

Witch-Hazel's own body felt like it would soon be torn apart by the now-deafening hum. She screamed, but the sound was swallowed into nothing beside the hum. She looked up at the ceiling of the rocky cavern, wishing she could see her home one more time before she died, but she was separated from the trees and sky by miles of rock and darkness. Yet it felt like an eye of the All-Being opened in the darkness above, stared down at the little squirrel unblinking, and acknowledged her terror.

"This way!" a tiny voice buzzed.

Was the All-Being speaking to her? Witch-Hazel wondered. *Answering her prayer?* How else could she have heard those words above the deafening hum? Then she felt a tickling sensation in her ear. A fuzzy yellow-and-black striped bee zipped away. The buzzing voice must have been it speaking from inside her own pointed ear.

The ground itself began shaking under Witch-Hazel's paws. The terrain shifted and shook. Rocks crumbled higher up the cavern and bounced downward, building to an avalanche. The castle rictus crumbled; its turret teeth fell out and tumbled into the lake. This cavern was folding in on itself.

Witch-Hazel had no better plan than to follow the inexplicable bee—yet another creature that didn't belong so far underground. She grabbed Fish-Breath's webbed paw with one of her own, and with her other paw, she gestured toward the bee. She shouted that they should follow it, but she couldn't even hear herself. There was no way that Fish-Breath or Twiggy could hear her. Still, she had their attention—between her wide tail flicking about like a flag in a storm, and her free paw pointing wildly at the air, trying to follow the jagged zigs and zags of the bee, she was making quite a scene. She couldn't tell if Fish-Breath understood her meaning, but he picked her up, swinging her into his arms and began trotting in the direction she pointed, along the coast of the lake.

Twiggy stuffed some of their supplies back into one of the frame packs, shouldered it onto her back, and scurried after them.

The bee flew in long swooping lines followed by sudden, swerving shifts in angle. Witch-Hazel wanted to look back at the sorcerer crabs to see if they were following or if they'd all been destroyed by the vibrations, but she couldn't take her eyes off the bee for a single second out of fear of losing track of it. All of her energy went into following the bee with her eyes, watching where it flew, and pointing toward it to guide Fish-Breath.

As they ran along the shore of the lake, the deafening hum shifted—it didn't exactly sound quieter, but the unpleasant thrumming it caused inside Witch-Hazel's chest subsided. The sound of the hum might have been quieter, but Witch-Hazel couldn't be sure, since it was supplemented now by the roar of rocks bouncing down the hillside.

The bee swooped suddenly backward, and Witch-Hazel flinched at the sight of its yellow stripes, gigantic in her face for a moment before it landed in her ear again.

Without Witch-Hazel's pointing to guide him, Fish-Breath stumbled to a halt.

Freed from the burden of watching the bee, Witch-Hazel glanced around the crumbling cavern. None of the sorcerer crabs were in sight, but the whole place was shaking. It wouldn't last much longer. The bee had led them to a thick column of stone that stretched up from the ground, all the way to the ceiling of the cavern. A stalactite and stalagmite that had joined together long ago. A doorway set in the column's base gaped open like a dark mouth.

The bee buzzed in Witch-Hazel's ear, "The way I came won't survive this rockslide. If we leave, we'll never make it back."

The deafening sound must have lessened, because Fish-Breath heard the bee and answered, "If we stay, we'll never survive. Lead on."

A booming crack resounded through the cavern, and the stone column in front of them split open. A jagged rip in the stone, shaped like a bolt of lightning, showed a spiral staircase hidden inside, now dangerously lopsided. The bottom half tilted leftward, and the top half tilted right. They met tenuously in the middle.

"Hurry!" the bee buzzed as she zipped through the now skewed doorway.

"Put me down," Witch-Hazel told Fish-Breath. Her leg had gone numb from the pain, and she found, testing it, that she could limp on it now. Even so, she needed to move faster than she could on a numb leg—or in the arms of a generous otter. Witch-Hazel reached into her knapsack, praying that the leontar's gift would be unbroken. She found the flask, uncorked it, and poured the red liquid down her throat, barely tasting its fiery sweetness. She didn't have time to worry about what exactly the potion would do, only to hope that it would help.

Once she'd licked the last sweet and sour drops out of the mouth of the flask, Witch-Hazel followed the others into the stairwell. She leaned her front paws against the wall, helping herself to hop up the steps, but she could already feel her injured leg growing stronger. Soon, she was hardly limping at all. Squirrels are good at climbing, and even limping, she raced ahead of her aquatic friends.

Round and round the spiral steps they hurried. The stone lurched beneath Witch-Hazel's paws, and her head slammed against the weirdly tilted wall beside her. Yet she gathered herself up and scurried on, dizzyingly upward. The stone continued swaying like a young tree in a windstorm, and Witch-Hazel's stomach tightened as she pictured the steps falling out from under her. They were higher up inside the cavern now than the tallest trees in her family's grove, but there were no branches to jump to here. A fall from this height down to the stone below would be catastrophic.

Yet for once, Witch-Hazel was traveling towards trees and sunlight instead of away from them, straight towards them, recovering ground in minutes that she'd spent hours slowly descending as they'd traveled down the meager slope of the cavern floor.

Witch-Hazel stopped to catch her breath and looked through a hole in the broken wall of the stairwell. She watched the shadowy cavern swallowing itself all around them. The castle, only dimly visible in the distance far below, was no longer a Halloween grin. It had become a twisted grimace, turrets broken, a toppled tower burning, and one end buried entirely in fallen boulders. As Witch-

Hazel watched, the castle's torches winked out and the burning tower succumbed to the suffocation of piles of falling stone, leaving the thundering, crumbling cavern in pitch blackness.

Twiggy rushed past Witch-Hazel, up the final steps of the spiral stair. From above the beaver squeaked, "There's a room up here where the ground feels stable! Hurry!"

Fish-Breath stopped beside Witch-Hazel and placed a webbed paw firmly on her back, pressing her to continue on.

13

As soon as their paws were on firm ground, the entrance to the spiral stair collapsed behind Witch-Hazel and Fish-Breath, sealing the mad crab sorcerers and the castle of the Order of Decapodia Crustacea forever in their underground grave. There would be no eternal river, and whatever celestial treasure had been hidden in the castle was lost to the little squirrel adventurer.

All of their quests had failed. Witch-Hazel was not a grand adventurer. Only a sad little squirrel with delusions of grandeur. And the Celestial Treasures were farther out of reach than any stash of buried hazelnuts had ever been. She'd never been able to find those, even when she'd been the one to bury them; it was pure folly to have imagined she'd do better when the stakes were higher.

Witch-Hazel heard the blubbery sound of an otter whimpering in the darkness beside her. She fumbled with her satchel and found the round gritty surface of a candle crystal.

Witch-Hazel slammed the candle crystal against the eerily steady floor, and flecks of blue glittered to light on the stone's surface. The soft glow filled the room. In the blue light, Witch-Hazel saw Fish-Breath wiping webbed-paws against his eyes, drying his tears, and Twiggy frowning angrily at the one frame pack she'd saved. The muslin sack was distressingly limp. The beaver had had little time to repack it when the avalanche started—only to throw a few things inside, strap the pack on her back and waddle, fast as she could, after Fish-Breath and the bee.

The bee—black, yellow, fuzzy, and many-legged—emerged from the muslin mouth of the frame pack and perched on one of its wooden crossbars. Her tiny multifaceted eyes glinted like obsidian in the blue light, and her antennae twitched, pointing at each of the mammals in turn. The bee was a creature of sunlight and flowers, and Witch-Hazel couldn't help feeling the tiny insect was even more out of place in this dark grave of a room than the rest of them.

"What were you doing in there?!" Twiggy grouched at the bee. The beaver shook the frame pack, jostling the bee into a buzzing flight.

Witch-Hazel flinched as the bee zoomed toward her, instinctually afraid of her sting, but the insect swerved away and landed on the cap of a fleshy pink toadstool. There were toadstools all around them in a fairy ring—the only distinguishing feature of the small dirt-walled room. Witch-Hazel didn't see an entrance or exit.

The bee preened her antennae with her two foremost limbs and sat cross-legged on the other four. Her obsidian eyes stared at Witch-Hazel piercingly, and the squirrel touched her chest to be sure the sunflower pendant was safely tucked away. It was. She wasn't sure she wanted the bee to know about it. And she was afraid that, somehow, the bee already did.

Still, stinger or no, the bee was so much smaller than Witch-Hazel, she couldn't truly feel threatened—even though the bee's stinger had clearly been sharpened. Normally, a honeybee couldn't sting more than once, but a sharpened stinger like that could sting over and over again. Ever since Witch-Hazel had let the singing snake send her on its fool's errand, she'd found herself judging every creature she met by how dangerous it was—who could kill whom if it came to a battle. She didn't like it, but she worried it would never go away.

"Can you get us out of here?" Witch-Hazel asked the bee. "Do you know the way back to the surface?" Even if the bee did know a direct route, Witch-Hazel worried they no longer had enough supplies to make it. A candle crystal had fallen out of her satchel during their mad dash through the avalanche, bringing her back down to two, and she didn't know if Twiggy had managed to save her mechanical torch.

"That six-legged devil flew out of the All-Being's castle!" Twiggy shrieked, buck teeth squealing. "What did you see in there? What caused this avalanche?"

Fish-Breath began to cry again.

The bee continued grooming her antennae, not deigning to address the beaver's aggrieved accusations.

"The All-Being destroyed the castle," Witch-Hazel said. "I prayed to the All-Being to save us, and the avalanche answered."

Fish-Breath's crying quieted, and between sobs, the otter asked, "The All-Being … doesn't want … the rivers restored? The All-Being doesn't want … us?" He got really quiet and finally added, "… me?"

Twiggy went over to her companion and embraced him. The otter melted into the beaver's arms, long spine bent over in a curve.

It broke Witch-Hazel's heart to see the usually happy otter so devastated. She came up and placed one of her small paws on his long back. She could feel the springy thickness of his fur through the wet fabric of his green jerkin. "I don't know what the All-Being wants," Witch-Hazel said, "but we want you. I want you to show me all the wonders of Riverton. I want to hear more of your stories, and I want you to teach me how to cook like you do. I want us all to get out of here alive."

"Restoring the river was always a long shot," Twiggy said. "We knew that."

"A dream," Fish-Breath whispered. He pulled himself together, straightened up, and said to the bee, "Thank you for saving us." He held out a webbed paw, as if to shake hands with the miniscule insect, although his paw dwarfed her entire body. "I'm Fish-Breath. My friends are Twiggy and Witch-Hazel." He gestured at the beaver and squirrel with his paw, unfazed by the bee's failure to shake it.

"My individuality is Zwitha Zo Zia, Fifth Handmaiden of the Second Hexagon, Daughter and Servant to Her Highness Queen Zewildra Zon Ziamon of the Purple Dogwood." Her antennae rotated in tiny circles. "You can call me Zwi."

The otter looked genuinely dazzled by the tiny handmaiden's introduction. Witch-Hazel, however, had already met a queen, king, and Sphynx in this underworld. The only thing the tiny insect could do to impress her was get them out of here.

"How did you get down here, Zwi?" Witch-Hazel wandered about the small room, avoiding the toadstools, and holding her glowing orb up to the walls. There was no obvious way out. A horrible thought occurred to her—the passage out could have collapsed with the cavern below. Then another horrible thought followed—the bee could have come down through a passage too small for the rest of them. She was so tiny.

Heavens above, this room truly was Witch-Hazel's grave, and she had to share it with a grumpy beaver, a heartbroken otter, and an ultimately useless bee. Was this truly what the All-Being had sent the avalanche for?

Oh no … What if the All-Being hadn't been answering Witch-Hazel's prayer? What if the bee really had caused the avalanche somehow? Or … maybe it was a completely natural avalanche.

Maybe there was no All-Being at all.

Everything the snake had sung was a lie. Lies hissed by a forked tongue.

And yet …

Had she not felt the eye of the All-Being look down on her as the avalanche began?

Witch-Hazel felt a webbed paw on her shoulder.

"Are you okay?" Fish-Breath asked. "You're shaking."

"More like vibrating," Twiggy said. "But that's normal for squirrels, right?"

"I think you're in shock from that cut to your leg." The otter leaned over to examine the jagged wound from the crab's pincer. "Wait," he said. "Is this the right leg?" He checked the other one. "It's gone! Did the All-Being heal you, too?"

"I drank a potion," Witch-Hazel said. "A gift from a Sphynx." Witch-Hazel tried to hold her tongue and sound brave for Fish-Breath, but her fear and bitterness overflowed: "Not that it will matter if we're trapped in here … I suppose we'll suffocate. Is that a bad way to die?" The air already felt warm and stuffy to her in their communal grave. If only she had found the Moon Opal, she wouldn't need the stuffy air. The Moon Opal's gift of endless breath would have let her live long enough to starve.

"Weren't you listening?" Twiggy said. "Your bee can get us out of here."

"I think she was too busy panicking," Fish-Breath said. "Explain it again, Zwi."

"I'll show instead," the bee buzzed, and then her delicate wings—transparent except for fine honey-colored veins—began flittering so fast they were a blur. She zipped from one toadstool to another in a complicated pattern. Her flight path sketched out a star-like shape in the air with each toadstool at a point of the star.

Slowly, the fleshy caps of the toadstools began to glow a soft pink, and Zwi's flight-path lit up in the air like a trail of embers. The bee's jagged path looked like dancing, and the hum of her wings sang a melody both enchanting and mysterious. Completely different from the snake's seductive song. Suddenly, with a flash and a snap, everything shifted—the dark walls of the tomb-like room were replaced with different walls and a darkness of a slightly different shade.

Zwi's flying slowed, and all four of them looked around. This time, there was a path out. Witch-Hazel jumped up, ready to skitter down the path and away from the bee's wild magic.

"Not here," Zwi buzzed. "I tried here before, and a monstrous earthworm nearly destroyed me." She began her ember-dance between the toadstools again.

Witch-Hazel had so many questions, she couldn't figure out which to ask. She was too hung up on the image of a monstrous earthworm, trying to figure out if, from Zwi's tiny perspective, a snake-sized earthworm was monstrous. Or if it was truly monstrous … were these tunnels made by a gigantic earthworm, large enough to dwarf a squirrel? And even an otter?

Even so, how could a useless, blind, fleshy tube destroy a stinger-wielding, flighted insect?

Another flash. Another snap. Another cave that Zwi deemed unacceptable before beginning her dance again.

Three caves later, the flashes of light glowed in Witch-Hazel's eyes like sunspots, and the snaps echoed in her ears.

"Wait," Witch-Hazel said to the zooming insect working her dizzying magic. "Don't you know where you're taking us? Are we anywhere near where we started?" They could have traveled across half the world by now. Witch-Hazel had no idea how far toadstool fairy rings could teleport them.

Zwi slowed down and hovered in the air in front of Witch-Hazel. The ember glow of her etched pentagrams drifted through the air, falling to the floor of this new cave where they flickered out. The toadstool fairy ring looked the same, but the stone walls here weren't the unformed, natural shape of the previous caves. The walls were straight and the corners square. This wasn't a cave; it was a chamber. And there was light coming from down a hallway.

The bee buzzed, "The Dances of the Underworld have been passed down through generations—from the hive in the Twin Oak to the hive in the Weeping Maple, the hive in the Flowering Cherry, all the way to the Purple Dogwood. They are folk tales. Of all my hive-sisters, only I believed that they could truly bring me to the Ancient Castle. So, no, I don't know where I'm taking you. I'm reading a map translated into an epic poem that then degraded into a lullaby for larva."

Zwi swooped and began flying in one of her archaic patterns again, but Witch-Hazel waved her paws and flicked her flag-like tail, shouting, "Stop! Stop!"

Zwi slowed and landed on one of the toadstools to watch the manic squirrel. The bee brushed a foreleg over each of her antennae, casual and calm. "Why?"

Witch-Hazel slipped her dimming candle crystal back into her satchel. Without the pale blue glow, the light from the end of the hall stood out more noticeably—a white light, plain and beckoning. Witch-Hazel pointed down the hallway. "Don't you want to know where that light's coming from?"

Both the otter and beaver looked curious, but the bee's expression was inscrutable. Her huge obsidian eyes and tightly closed mandibles revealed nothing of her emotions.

Witch-Hazel continued, "Or have you been here before? Is that the work-light in the drawing room of another monstrous earthworm?"

"No," Zwi buzzed primly. "I have not been to this cave before."

"Then what's wrong with it?" Witch-Hazel pressed.

"It's not where I came from. I won't be able to find my way home."

"Where you came from?" Witch-Hazel chittered angrily. "None of these places are where I came from! There were no fairy rings of toadstools ANYWHERE on my way down!"

The beaver and otter watched wide-eyed as the little squirrel shouted at an even tinier bee.

"No matter where you teleport us, I'm still lost." Witch-Hazel turned to her mammalian companions. "What about you? Did you pass one of these toadstool rings on your way down?"

Both the otter and beaver shook their heads.

"We're all lost," Witch-Hazel said. "We have to accept that. At this point, we have to focus on getting back to the surface. Anywhere with sunlight." Witch-Hazel walked out of the fairy ring and held out a paw toward Fish-Breath. The otter took it. Twiggy followed too. "We're going to find our way to the surface," Witch-Hazel said, glancing back at the bee. "You're welcome to join us."

The bee buzzed fitfully, undecidedly behind them as Witch-Hazel led her friends away.

14

THE STONE UNDERFOOT CHANGED, growing smoother, as they proceeded down the hall. After a turn, they found the source of the light—a flickering lantern, hung carefully from a hook in the wall. Its single flame, housed inside four panels of glass, swayed at their approach, threatening to snuff out. Under its light, Witch-Hazel noticed ornate tile patterns on the hallway floor. Blue swirls and yellow flecks conjured images of windy skies and twilight fireflies to Witch-Hazel. She felt the seams between the tiles under her tired paws. They felt civilized compared to the rough, unhewn floors they'd trod for days now.

They stumbled down one hallway to the next. Some halls had lanterns. Some were dark. When they reached a fork in the path, Witch-Hazel hesitated. If Zwi followed them, she wouldn't know which way they'd gone unless they left some sort of clue on the floor. Witch-Hazel sifted through her backpack. She'd already used up the witch hazel leaves on various injuries, and everything else was food—mostly mushrooms gathered from the previous cavern. Since there weren't any mushrooms growing here,

Witch-Hazel was reluctant to leave any behind. The way she figured it, there was already a good chance that she, Fish-Breath, and Twiggy would starve before they found a way to the surface. She couldn't spare any mushrooms.

Besides, Zwi might not even understand the signal if she did leave one.

"You okay?" Fish-Breath asked, uncertain why Witch-Hazel had stopped.

"I don't know which way to go," she admitted. "And when we do pick, what if Zwi can't find us?"

"We go up," Twiggy said. "Obviously."

"Don't worry about Zwi," Fish-Breath said. "She can take care of herself."

Witch-Hazel couldn't argue with that. Zwi had gotten all the way down to the castle entirely on her own, and her toadstool magic was pretty impressive. Witch-Hazel wondered what other magic the bee might have, and how long she'd been at the castle. Maybe she'd seen the Star Sliver or the Moon Opal hidden there. Unfortunately, Witch-Hazel hadn't had a chance to ask, and now she might not see the bee again.

But Witch-Hazel had abandoned that quest, exactly as she'd feared she would. She had a different one to focus on now. "Which way is up?" she asked. "They both look the same to me." On her way down, the slant of the tunnels had always been obvious. Here, though, Witch-Hazel was lost.

"Leave that to Twiggy!" Fish-Breath proclaimed proudly.

The beaver dropped a small round pebble on the ground several times, testing the slope of the floor on either branch of the hall. "The right path slants up more than the left one. It's our best bet for heading towards the surface." The beaver's whiskers twitched as she sniffed the air, as if trying to smell the sunlight and grass hidden far above.

Witch-Hazel could almost smell it too. She swooned against Fish-Breath. She was feeling faint; whatever energy the potion had used to heal her body had left her exhausted. There couldn't be fresh grass to smell down here, and she had to be imagining the faint whispered hiss of the snake's song.

"Let's find a place to rest," Witch-Hazel said.

Past two more forks where Twiggy tested for the better path, the hallway opened into a chamber. As soon as Witch-Hazel stepped through the door, she felt the change in the air. The openness of the room vibrated in her whiskers. More than a room, it was a balcony, overlooking another great cavern like the one they'd left crumbling behind them.

Witch-Hazel ran to the edge of the balcony, leaned over the balustrade, and looked deep into the darkness of the scooped-out hollow, a giant pocket of air buried inside miles and miles of rock. There was no castle in this cavern, only mounds of rocks far below the balcony. Witch-Hazel wondered why anyone would build a balcony to look out on such a plain scene, and then she turned her gaze directly down. There was her answer: peeking out from the piles of scree, she saw the turret-teeth of the castle. The same castle.

This was the cavern they'd been in before, seen from a different angle.

"I know where we are," Witch-Hazel said. "We're within sight of where we used to be."

Fish-Breath leaned over the balustrade beside her, but then he backed away quickly, stifling a sniffle.

A buzzing joined them from behind, and Witch-Hazel looked back to see Zwi zigging and zagging through the air.

"We are still lost," the bee said.

"How did you find us?" Witch-Hazel asked, ready to marvel at another insectoid feat of magic. "There were so many twists and turns."

"I followed …" Zwi hesitated. "… your vibrations. I felt them in the air." She waved her antennae meaningfully.

"What changed your mind?" Twiggy asked with a toothy whistle.

"After dancing through a few more fairy rings," Zwi buzzed, "I found the chamber I was looking for—the way

I came down before, but the way out was blocked. It must have collapsed in the rockslide. "

"We're all lost now." The otter's voice was hauntingly bleak and despairing. "None of us know the way out."

"We'll find it," Witch-Hazel insisted. Her companions, even the bee with those inscrutable obsidian eyes and mandibles, looked doubtful.

Witch-Hazel dug through her knapsack to the very bottom where the flask of her sister's pear cider had settled. It was barely a quarter full—just enough for each of them to drink a quick swig. Witch-Hazel was loath to share it. If they didn't find their way out of here, then these drops would be the last taste of her sister's cider she'd ever have … But she couldn't let herself think that way.

Witch-Hazel unscrewed the cap, gulped down a mouthful of the sweet liquor, and then held the flask out to Fish-Breath. "Go on," she said. "Consider it a toast—to being saved by the All-Being, and honoring our rescue by getting out of this dark and gloomy underworld!"

Fish-Breath still looked unsure, but Twiggy said, "I'll drink to that!" The beaver took the flask, quaffed half of what remained, and then shoved the flask into the otter's webbed paws. "And you'll drink to it, too."

Fish-Breath smiled weakly at his friend. The otter and beaver had a bond that Witch-Hazel envied. She wanted friendship like that.

Fish-Breath nearly finished the flask. He set it down on the balcony floor for Zwi, and the bee landed on its round mouth. She was just the right size to crawl inside to get to the drops left at the bottom. When the bee crawled back out, her antennae were verily spinning. Witch-Hazel could have sworn she saw the little bee hiccough.

The tired band of doomed animals chased their mouthfuls of pear cider with a snack of wrinkly dried mushrooms and some scratchy stale bread that had survived in Twiggy's frame pack. Zwi provided a single dewdrop-sized bead of honey for each piece of bread from a tiny backpack she wore between her wings. It wasn't more than a taste, but the sweetness of the honey exploded on Witch-Hazel's tongue like sunlight bursting through the clouds on a rainy day. The flavor fortified her, and the weight of the bread and mushrooms in her belly sated her. They weren't much, but she'd been eating so little lately, even a modest snack filled her belly like a feast. She tried not to think of those mushrooms and bread as her last meal. Yet she knew how little food she had left in her knapsack.

After their snack, the group of four followed the balcony as it curved around the edge of the cavern, overlooking the scene of such recent destruction. The balcony was long with many doorways leading back into the warren of tunnels that had apparently always riddled the ground beneath Witch-Hazel's home forest. She'd never imagined the underworld like this. It had seemed solid and anchoring from above. Down here, it was like a honeycomb—intricate, complex, and easily crushed by underground avalanches.

Eventually they came to the end of the balcony. The balustrade swelled outward and then back up to the rock wall, closing the balcony off. The narrow balcony widened into a round terrace with a hole in the middle. A single tree grew up through that hole, its trunk encircled by the balcony. The tree's branches stretched toward a sky they would never reach, let alone see. Yet here it was—without sunlight, without rain, somehow the tree persisted in this dark cavern, adorned with pink flowers, glowing like a sunset.

It was the magnolia tree from the medallion puzzle. Witch-Hazel was sure of it.

"I know this tree," she said. "It's important." She shouldered off her knapsack and satchel, dropped them on the floor, and let her squirrel instincts take over. Her heart beat like a clarion call, propelling her toward the magnolia's inviting trunk. The moment her claws sank into the woody bark, she felt like she was home again. She scurried up the tree's trunk, circling it as she climbed.

Witch-Hazel climbed high into the magnolia's crown, skittering along the branches, jumping from one to the next, until she was so high that the branches had grown as thin as her own limbs and swayed with her weight. It felt natural. It felt right. She could almost forget the days of darkness, both the days behind and the days ahead. When she closed her eyes, Witch-Hazel could almost feel the warmth of sunlight on her pointed ears and the stirring of a summer breeze in the long fur of her tail.

Witch-Hazel clung to the narrow branch, and her heart slowed. She felt peaceful, safe. If she were going to die underground, she'd rather die here. With her eyes closed. Feeling magnolia bark beneath her claws and the bobbing sway of a branch, rocking her, comforting her, transporting her home, if only in her imagination.

"Witch-Hazel?" the otter called from the balcony's floor. "Is there something important in the tree? What do you mean it's important?"

"*Every tree is important,*" Witch-Hazel whispered to herself.

An answer buzzed in her ear, "This one is particularly important, isn't it? You know—"

Witch-Hazel opened her eyes, reluctantly, to see the tiny bee buzzing circles around her.

"—about the Celestial Fragments, don't you?" The bee landed on a waxy pink flower petal. "We're on the same quest, aren't we?"

"*My quest is to get my friends home.*" Witch-Hazel grimaced at the lie—here she clung to a tree branch, ready to give up and die, and yet she still claimed to care about saving Fish-Breath and Twiggy.

"You're gathering the Celestial Fragments," Zwi buzzed, running a tiny hook-like claw over one of her antennae. "And you already have one of them, don't you?"

Before she could stop herself, Witch-Hazel let go of the branch with one forepaw and touched her breast to feel the sunflower pendant hidden there. She bristled at her own unconscious action, revealing her secret in spite of herself. And yet clearly, the bee already knew.

"You were in the castle," Witch-Hazel said. "Did you find a fragment there?" Her voice was a whisper, loud enough for Zwi to hear but much too quiet to carry down the trunk of the tree to their other companions.

"Show me yours," Zwi buzzed.

"I don't have one," Witch-Hazel said.

"Liar. What kind of vibrations do you think I was following to find you in this labyrinth? My kind navigate by the sun. You carry the Sun Shard, and it calls to me."

"What if I do?" Witch-Hazel's gray fur bristled all over her body, feeling prickly against her clothes, and her tail whipped about erratically, displaying all her chaotic emotions far too plainly, yet she couldn't control it. The sunflower pendant felt like it was burning against her chest. She filled with excitement, realizing she'd been carrying one of the Celestial Fragments with her for so long, and also a confusing shame that she hadn't been clever enough to realize it.

"I need it for my queen," Zwi buzzed. "She's ... dying."

The bee's obvious distress—the way her antennae bent forward and her translucent wings drooped—touched Witch-Hazel. In the snake's song and the stories from her childhood, the Sun Shard granted strength. A definite boon to a dying queen. Besides Witch-Hazel didn't even know why she wanted it anymore. She couldn't ascend to the All-Being's realm in the sky without all three of the fragments, and one of them must be buried deep under a landslide now. Even if Zwi had seen it while she was in the castle, there'd be no way to get to it again, and even though the bee had a tiny backpack nestled between her wings, it couldn't be large enough to hold one of the missing Celestial Fragments. Whatever treasure Zwi had seen in the castle was surely buried beyond recovery now.

Even so, Witch-Hazel envied Zwi's possible brush with the second missing Fragment. "I have the Sun Shard," Witch-Hazel admitted. "It was a gift to me from another queen ... Amalah the Salamander from the Fire Realm ..." Witch-Hazel lost herself in the memory of that tiny regal squiggle of a creature—strangely silly and yet fiercely terrifying. Perhaps a gift from a queen should be passed on to another queen. "Tell me though, was it the Star Sliver or the Moon Opal in the castle? And what did it look like? I can hardly believe it's lost forever ..." Her gaze strayed to the turret-teeth jutting out of the landslide in the dark distance.

"Lost?" Zwi's antennae wiggled and her wings fluttered in amusement. "The Moon Opal is safely tucked into that beaver's frame pack. You don't think I would have flown away without it?"

Witch-Hazel closed her eyes and tried to remember the moment she first saw Zwi—had the bee been carrying something in her six limbs? Witch-Hazel didn't think so. But there had been sorcerer crabs with water whips chasing her, and the ground itself had been shaking like it meant to open up and swallow her into a fiery, lava-filled center of the Earth. She couldn't trust her own memories.

"That means …" Witch-Hazel was almost afraid to say the words. She'd already given up on this quest. "… we could still find all three. We could still ascend to meet the All-Being."

"One of us could," Zwi agreed archly.

"Only one of us," Witch-Hazel said the words slowly, letting the sharpness of their truth penetrate her.

"Why do you seek audience with the All-Being?" Zwi asked, judgment filling her tiny buzzing voice.

"To …" Witch-Hazel fumbled and started again. "Because …" After a few more stutters, she had to admit, "I don't know." But she turned the question right back to Zwi, expecting a similarly facile answer: "Why do you?"

"My queen is dying."

Angry and frustrated that the bee's reason was so much more selfless than hers, Witch-Hazel argued, "And you expect the All-Being to—what? Save her?"

"I expect guidance," Zwi buzzed. Her antennae drooped. "I was sent to scout out a new home, a place for a new hive. The purple dogwood—its heart and my queen's heart are tied together. When they die, we'll have no more home."

"There are trees everywhere," Witch-Hazel chittered. "Why do you need guidance from the All-Being?"

Zwi's antennae quivered and dipped even lower over her triangular face. "Our home tree has always been blessed by the All-Being—kissed by sunlight, soothed by breezes sent by the All-Being." Zwi's buzzing voice turned hollow. "But the All-Being no longer speaks to us, and we do not know which trees are consecrated by the All-Being's touch anymore. We do not know where to live when our dogwood dies."

Witch-Hazel tried to imagine believing her family's copse of trees were somehow inspirited by the All-Being's touch—a touch they felt they needed. She almost could. When her mother had died, it had felt like the soul had gone out of all the trees. She'd felt alone and lost, even surrounded by sisters and brothers, even among the trees that had always been her home.

"I'll help you find the Star Sliver and let you use all three Fragments to reach the All-Being if you promise to ask about the eternal river." She glanced down between the branches of the magnolia tree to glimpse Twiggy and Fish-Breath, obscured by all the clusters of pink petals, far below. She tried to think of what her otter friend would ask the All-Being if he were the one to ascend. "Why did it dry up? Can it be started again? I don't know what you should ask—but promise you'll carry whatever question Fish-Breath sends with you, and I'll help you be the one that ascends to meet the All-Being."

Still perched on the pink petal, Zwi bent four of her legs in an elaborate curtsey. "That is more than fair," she buzzed. "You are a kind and generous squirrel. My hive will dance waltzes in your name for generations to come."

The idea of a Witch-Hazel Waltz tickled the squirrel, and she chittered happily. Still, there was work to be done. "Go get the Moon Opal, and I'll look for the Star Sliver."

15

Zwi flew back down to the terrace, and Witch-Hazel scurried over the branches of the magnolia tree, circling the woody limbs and feeling for oddities in the way they swayed beneath her—a heavier or hollow limb could hide the treasure she sought, but they all bounced and waved just as they should. She jumped from one to the next, and worked her way around the tree until she was sure she'd set claw to bark in every major branch. None of the branches moved like they had something to hide.

Witch-Hazel turned her attention to the magnolia's heart—the place where the trunk of the tree split into three wide, winding branches.

Witch-Hazel scratched at the gray-brown bark, leaving bright lines of sap. She expected a knothole or tiny door embedded in the trunk, hiding the Star Sliver inside. But found nothing. Just tree.

Zwi came buzzing back from the terrace below where Twiggy and Fish-Breath were resting, unaware of the excitement above. In her six claws, she held a milky gemstone set in a silver ring. The gem was blue and yellow and pink all at once, and its surface was perfectly smooth. No facets, not like the topaz in the sunflower pendant Witch-Hazel wore.

Of course, the gem in the sunflower pendant wasn't a topaz at all. It never had been. It was the Sun Shard, a broken fragment of the sun. No wonder it had helped her prayer rise up to the All-Being.

Witch-Hazel pulled the pendant out from her jacket and let the golden sunflower swing, spinning lightly on its chain. The Sun Shard in the middle twinkled and winked brightly, much more brightly than it had any right to do this deep underground in a dim cave.

It shone with its own light.

The light of the sun.

And the Moon Opal answered with a sleepy gleam.

Zwi landed on the wrinkly bark and turned the milky gemstone over in her claws. The silver ring it was set into would slip over one of Witch-Hazel's paw pads loosely. On Zwi, it was large enough to be a heavy, oversized crown. It was beautiful, full of nighttime and mystery the way that the Sun Shard burst with noontime blaze and summer heat.

"We're so close," Witch-Hazel said. "But I can't find the Star Sliver." She wished there was another queen here to hand it to her, the way that Amalah the salamander queen had.

Zwi lifted a claw from holding the Moon Opal to point at the Sun Shard hanging from Witch-Hazel's neck. "Look," she buzzed.

Witch-Hazel looked down and saw that the pendant wasn't hanging straight. It pulled to the side, drawn by an unseen force. She followed the gentle tug at the end of the pendant's chain. It led her along one of the branches, up and out of the heart and into the crown of the magnolia tree. She stepped lightly, carefully as the branch stretched out to a mere twig, bending under her weight. Eventually, the sunflower pendant bumped against a closed flower—a half dozen waxy-pink petals smugly folded up like a tulip. But at the touch of the sunflower pendant, the petals uncurled, and a sparkling point of light floated inside with a delicate filigree of silver chain trailing beneath it.

"The Star Sliver," Witch-Hazel breathed. She was almost afraid to touch it, so surreal was the way it floated above the now-unfolded magnolia flower.

"What's going on?" an otter voice called from below, curious.

"What's so interesting in that tree?" The beaver voice sounded less curious, more impatient.

Witch-Hazel lifted the golden chain from around her neck and held it out toward Zwi. The bee hovered in the air, swaying back and forth, beside the similarly hovering Star Sliver. The golden pendent swung toward the Star Sliver, and the two Celestial Fragments brushed against each other like a kiss. Star gleam and sunbeam burst from their touch in a flash.

"How do we do this?" Witch-Hazel asked, dazzled by the magic light. She wondered, if she held on to the golden chain, and Zwi wore the ring like a crown … Could they both ascend to meet the All-Being? But Zwi had seemed so sure that it could be only one of them. Besides if Witch-Hazel ascended, she'd leave her new friends, Twiggy and Fish-Breath, behind. She wanted to see them safely to the surface. She wanted them to show her Riverton.

Witch-Hazel carefully placed the golden chain inside the magnolia flower. It twined with the Star Sliver's silver chain, gold and silver twisting together, and the Celestial Fragments themselves brushed and bumped each other, kissing and flashing with tantalizing magical light as they floated above the pink petals.

"Wear the ring like a crown," Witch-Hazel said.

The little bee placed the silver circle over her antennae. She looked like a tiny queen wearing the heavy crown. She flew toward the other Celestial Fragments, and when all three touched, a burst of light, colorful and complicated, danced like an aurora borealis above the pink petals, clothing the little bee in a rainbow glow.

"What is that?!" Twiggy called from below. "What did you find?"

"Wait!" Witch-Hazel said in a panic, remembering that Zwi hadn't asked Fish-Breath for a question to pass along to the All-Being yet. Her heart skipped. Was it too late?

But the dancing lights continued to dance. Nothing more happened.

"I think ..." Zwi buzzed. "We're too deep underground. They need sunlight to work."

The bee knew so much more about the Celestial Fragments than Witch-Hazel did. That snake's song had sent her on a quest completely unprepared.

Witch-Hazel plucked the sunflower pendant from where it floated in the air and hung it around her neck again. "I can keep the other two in my knapsack," she said.

Zwi lifted the ring from her triangular head with her foremost pair of limbs and offered the silver circlet to the squirrel. Witch-Hazel tucked both the ring and the circlet into a secure pocket in her knapsack.

She felt a swell of pride—she had succeeded; she was the greatest treasure hunter of all the squirrels she knew! "Now let's get back to our friends, and find a way up to the sunlight," she said. "As quickly as possible."

"Should we tell them about the Fragments?" Zwi asked.

"I don't know," Witch-Hazel said. She remembered squabbles among her siblings where troves of chestnuts were concerned. Sisters and brothers fighting tooth and nail, fluffy tails bleeding and chunks of fur flying. If sharing a few shiny nuts could cause such fights, how much more trouble could this magical treasure trove cause? "Maybe not."

"I'll follow your lead," Zwi buzzed.

Witch-Hazel's heart swelled even further. She'd never been a leader before, but down here in the dark, she felt like she'd finally found herself. And when it was needed, she could find treasure, and she could lead.

Witch-Hazel spiraled her way down the magnolia tree's trunk, savoring every touch of the blessed bark beneath her claws—it felt so much more natural than unyielding stone or shifty dirt. Firm but giving. Witch-Hazel was loath to place her paws on the ground again, but the sight of the Fragments' dancing lights had given her hope. She would get her friends back to the surface. She would make it back to her family's grove soon. And then Riverton!

At the base of the magnolia, Witch-Hazel greeted her friends with the words: "I had a vision of the All-Being." It was only partly a lie—those rainbow lights had been a glimpse of the All-Being's power.

Zwi buzzed down from the magnolia's hallowed branches as if drifting on a phantom summer breeze and landed on the ground beside Witch-Hazel's left paw.

"What did the All-Being say?" Fish-Breath asked, whiskers quivering. His wide otter face was strangely somber and serious.

"It wasn't like that ..." Witch-Hazel fumbled. "Only a glimpse. No words."

Zwi buzzed: "It was more like a feeling—the All-Being is guiding us, back to the sunlight."

Fish-Breath broke into a wide otter grin and repeated the words, "Back to the sunlight," quietly, reverently.

Twiggy gave the squirrel and bee a skeptical stare, but Witch-Hazel didn't flinch. At some level, she did believe the All-Being was guiding them. Why else had the snake sung to her? Why else had the avalanche brought her and Zwi together, each with their own Fragments? Why else had she stepped out of the fairy ring, following a lantern's light, only to be drawn here, to the final Fragment?

"If the All-Being is guiding us," Fish-Breath said, "then we should get our tails shaking!" He looked at the bee and asked, "Do you have a tail? Make that, tails and stingers!"

Zwi chuckled, a tiny trilling buzz, and Witch-Hazel realized she'd never heard a bee laugh before. There was so much left to discover in this world, and she would discover it. After her successful quest underground, she could achieve anything.

Witch-Hazel shook her spectacular tail, and the long gray fur shimmered like a silver waterfall in the dim cave light. Her little dance drew a deep-bellied guffaw from Fish-Breath and a slight smile from Twiggy. "Like you said, let's get our tails shaking!" Then she set off—back into the honeycomb labyrinth of passages, leading up and away from the cavern of the landslide-buried castle. She'd already found all the treasure she needed down here—Celestial Fragments and new friends. All she had left to do was get back to the sun.

As they traveled, Fish-Breath told stories again, and when they stopped to rest, he did what cooking he could with the remaining dried mushrooms and bits of smoked fish that he'd had stowed away in hidden pockets of his jerkin. Witch-Hazel had never eaten fish before. The flavor was strange and overpowering, but she thought that anything might taste good to her now. Nevertheless she began to think of Fish-Breath as a wizard of cookery. She wondered what he could do with a full stash of gleaming chestnuts and dusky acorns.

Every time they came to a branch in the paths, Twiggy measured which fork sloped upward. Though sometimes Zwi insisted she could feel the pull of the sun more strongly coming from the other way. At first Twiggy objected, but Witch-Hazel insisted they follow Zwi's instincts. Fish-Breath backed her up. The otter was completely dazzled by the story Witch-Hazel and Zwi had told of their vision in the magnolia tree. They had to tell him again and again of how the rainbow lights had radiated the All-Being's love, protection, and guidance. They didn't even have to ask what question he would want carried to the All-Being—it was almost all he could talk about, everything he'd say to the All-Being if he could.

And it all came back to: "Where did the waters of the endless river go? When the river dried up, where did the waters go?"

When they stopped to sleep in the stone passageways, Twiggy folded her wide, flat tail under her like a sleeping mat, and Zwi crawled inside the frame pack. The sleeping bags were long gone, lost in the avalanche. Without even discussing it, Fish-Breath and Witch-Hazel curled up together, sharing the warmth of their bodies against the cold of the stone beneath them. His fur was thick and dense, and the way his long body curled around hers made Witch-Hazel feel safe. She hoped they would continue to travel together for a long time after emerging back into the sunlight. She wanted him to stay with her, and she thought that, if she asked, he probably would.

After three nights—measured only by when the group grew too tired to trek onward—they came to another heavy wooden door decorated with a metal medallion. This time only one—large, round, and gold with tiny depictions of the sun, constellations of stars, and phases of the moon etched all around its circumference.

Witch-Hazel didn't wait for Twiggy to crack it. She went right up to the gold medallion and turned it until the noon-day sun sat at the top. With a slight shove of her paws, the door swung open.

A rush of fresh air streamed through her whiskers, and Witch-Hazel imagined she heard a susurrus, a lilting strain of whispered song. The snake's song, inviting her back to the world above. She shivered.

16

Twiggy pushed past the others and entered the new chamber first. Her sundress was tattered and dingy from their travels, and her brown fur was thick with grease and dust. The mostly-empty frame pack weighed heavily on her hunched shoulders, but her demeanor changed, her back straightened out, as she entered the room. Her small round ears turned about, listening in every direction, betraying her excitement. Her teeth whistled as she said, "It's a library. I've never seen so many books before …"

Witch-Hazel followed the dumbstruck beaver into the new chamber. It put the library in the mole city to shame. Shelf after shelf, floor to towering ceiling, stretching all along the hallway and branching into row after row of hallways, all of them crammed tightly with brightly bound books, lit by glimmering candles. This was not an abandoned library. Someone cared for these books, kept them dusted and loved, and had carefully lit every one of these candles.

They were no longer lost in abandoned caverns. They had found their way to some form of civilization.

Overcome, Witch-Hazel called out: "Hello! Is there anyone here? A librarian?"

Her chittery voice echoed among the books, and a cawing voice answered.

"*Intruders! Book thieves!*"

The candles all flickered under the wind of flapping black wings. Ebony feathers and a blue brocade cape swept down from the high ceiling. The raven sporting the feathers and brocade had a crazy gleam in her dark eyes; her beak was sharp and pointed like an obsidian dagger. She clacked it menacingly and squawked, "None of these books will ever leave the premises! Away ye thieves!"

The raven grabbed a decorative iron vine that twisted upward between two of the bookcases with her talons, flapped her wings a final time, and settled into her eerily sideways perch. Though her body was sideways, she tilted her feathered head to look at the small gang of intruders straight on.

On a different journey, in a different lifetime, with more food in her belly and a clear vision of the path back to the world of sunlight, Witch-Hazel would have loved to read these books. But the grueling nature of their journey, the uncertainty that they'd even survive, had driven curiosity out of her. All she had left was the drive to bring her friends, still alive, back to the surface. And sunlight.

"We don't want your books," Witch-Hazel said, summoning the courage to step forward and speak to the bird. The feathered librarian was easily as large as her, and its beak and talons looked far more dangerous than her modest claws and teeth. Also, the look in its eyes reminded her of Salal-Berry. Here was another creature of the sky who had spent far, far too long underground. "All we want is a way back to the surface. Do you know the way up? Are ..." She faltered, voice breaking over the importance of the question. "Are we close?"

Witch-Hazel's fluffy tail flicked wildly, betraying the urgency of her emotions. For all she knew, Twiggy's calculations and Zwi's intuition were nothing but superstitions, leading them in circles or, worse, deeper underground.

"Oh, yes," the raven cawed. "Quite close."

Witch-Hazel felt the slight weight of Zwi landing on her shoulder and the press of Fish-Breath's webbed paw on her back. Twiggy slapped her broad tail on the floor three times like a triumphant tattoo of a drum. Her companions radiated relief, but Witch-Hazel wasn't ready to believe the words of a mad underground bird just yet. "How close?" she asked.

"Two spiral stairs to the top of the library," the raven cawed. For a moment, Witch-Hazel's heart leapt, imagining the surface so close. Then the raven continued, "After that, one level of the old church catacombs, and then the church itself. It was buried by infidel lizards." The raven hissed those final words, conveying every scrap of contempt that two words could.

Witch-Hazel liked the sound of neither catacombs nor infidel lizards. In fact, she didn't see how catacombs sounded different than the passages they'd been wandering since leaving the magnolia tree. "Can you guide us?" she asked the raven. She wasn't sure she wanted to add the raven to their merry band of lost souls, but she also didn't like the idea of traveling onwards without it—leaving that beak, those talons, and the madly gleaming eyes behind her tail. Possibly following her.

"Yes," the raven cawed. "*But no books!*" The ebony-feathered librarian punctuated her admonishment with widespread wings and a twist of her head to the other side, causing her to look at the rest of them upside down. "All the books stay here."

Twiggy muttered something that may have included the words, *crazy*, *bird*, and *no one wants your books*. Fortunately, the crazy bird didn't seem to care about the beaver's words, only that she put the thick red-bound tome she'd been examining back on its shelf.

"Follow, follow," the raven cawed, taking to wing again and flapping through the suddenly narrow-seeming halls of books. Zwi flew after the raven, following the bird's erratic zigging and zagging as though they were riding the same invisible zephyr. Bee and bird, flying along underground. The squirrel, otter, and beaver scampered after them as quickly as possible by paw.

They scurried past more books than Witch-Hazel could read in a lifetime. More books than she'd ever imagined. Books that could have told her entire life story, and the life stories of all of her friends and littermates, and all of their families for generations-past. Enough books to hold every recipe Fish-Breath could ever invent, the schematics for every gadget Twiggy could ever build, and the words to every song any snake could ever sing.

The sight of all of those books, carefully organized, lined up on their shelves, daunted Witch-Hazel. She felt small in a way that not even the sight of the All-Being's wide eye looking down on her as the avalanche began had made her feel.

Perhaps, if there were so many words that animals had found worth writing, so much to say and preserve, this world was too big for even an All-Being to oversee.

As promised, the raven librarian led them up a spiral staircase, past many more shelves of books, and then up a second spiral of stairs. Finally, they were traveling clearly upward, instead of agonizing over imperceptibly different slopes of otherwise identical passageways.

At the top of the second stair, the raven turned to face her followers and landed on the ground. She drew a glinting silver key out of a pocket in her blue brocade cape. The key dangled from her talon on a yellow ribbon and swayed, mesmerizingly. A promise of possible freedom. "Before you go," the raven cawed, "answer one riddle."

Witch-Hazel thought back to the leontaur and supposed that she was about due for a mad creature asking her a riddle. At least this time, the creature was small enough that her gang might be able to hold it down and steal the key if they got the riddle wrong.

The raven hopped, balancing on one talon, the other still holding the tantalizing, swaying key. "What brought you to my library?"

"Is that a riddle?" Witch-Hazel asked.

All the raven said in response was, "Answer it, and we'll see."

Twiggy said, "My otter friend and I were on a quest to restore the endless river."

Zwi buzzed, "A quest on behalf of my hive queen."

The raven stared at Witch-Hazel until she reluctantly added, "I was sent on a quest by a singing snake." As she said the words, once again, she thought she heard a waft of the snake's song hissing through the air.

"And did you complete your quests?" the raven cawed, tilting her head to the side.

The otter and beaver said, "No," at the same time but with varying degrees of heartbreak and despondence.

Zwi and Witch-Hazel looked at each other, but the squirrel still couldn't read the bee's expression on her triangular face. She'd said she would follow Witch-Hazel's lead, and the truth was—even though they had the Celestial Fragments hidden away—the bee's quest wouldn't be complete until she used them. Witch-Hazel had completed her quest. She'd found the treasures. But that was secret. This raven didn't need to know.

Witch-Hazel chittered, "No," and the bee buzzed the same a moment later.

The raven squawked, an irate, inchoate sound. She flapped her wings, hopped again, and shifted her hold on the yellow ribbon, pulling the key itself up into her fierce claw.

She unlocked the door.

"Get out of my library," the raven cawed, her voice grown rougher, hoarser, thick with an indecipherable emotion.

Twiggy and Fish-Breath thanked the raven and hurried through the wooden door, out of the library and into the church catacombs. Zwi buzzed after them. Witch-Hazel followed, but as soon as she passed the threshold of the door, the raven cawed, quietly, in her ear, "*Never return, and may the snake give you what you deserve. Liar.*"

Witch-Hazel whirled about to face the mad raven, but the wooden door slammed in her face. She heard the mechanism clink back into a locked state.

Witch-Hazel was filled with a mad desire to break down the wooden door and scream at the bird to tell her what it had meant. She wanted to claw and scrabble at the wood, run and throw her shoulder against it. But instead, she turned to see her companions already rushing onward through a stone passageway with shelf-like ledges on the sides where skeletons of all variety of species rested, reposed in a final sleep.

Witch-Hazel's fur rose, prickling out, as she followed her companions. She passed mole, ferret, beaver, otter, fox, and even squirrel skeletons, carefully arranged with their paws crossed over their empty rib cages. The hollows of their eye sockets stared blindly upward.

"Is this a church of the All-Being?" Witch-Hazel called out.

Fish-Breath turned back, many paces ahead, and called back to her, "Must be. What else could it be?"

Witch-Hazel feared to imagine an answer to that question.

"Hurry up!" Twiggy added. "The sooner we make the surface, the sooner we can find a river to soak in."

"Water in my fur!" Fish-Breath agreed. "That's what I need more than anything!"

"Trees and sunlight …" Witch-Hazel chittered to herself. Then she hurried after the others, trying not to imagine the skeletons rising behind her as undead warriors intent on her dismemberment.

Or maybe just their ghosts, ephemeral and wicked, whisking after her like a toxic breeze.

Witch-Hazel turned a corner, and the narrow corridor lined with shelves of skeletons was replaced with a large, open room filled with free-standing sarcophagi. Each stone tomb was decorated with intricate carvings, and their heavy lids featured chiseled portraits of scaly lizards and twisting snakes. "They're all decorated with reptiles," Witch-Hazel said. "Why?"

A breath of air sighed through the room of sarcophagi, tickling the fur on Witch-Hazel's neck and stirring the long silver hairs of her tail. She heard the snake's song in the distance, but closer than last time.

"The Cult of the Second Awakening," Twiggy said, with a whistle from between her teeth. The beaver had stopped beside one of the smaller sarcophagi. Her paws rested on the edge of its heavy lid. "Reptiles who believe that death—for them—is only hibernation until the All-Being awakens them. They're dead inside this tomb, but according to their religion, they're only sleeping."

"So, it is a church of the All-Being." Witch-Hazel's tail flicked restlessly. She wished the strains of the snake's hissing song would leave her ears alone. She wanted to stuff them full of crumpled oak leaves. She couldn't wait to feel live oak leaves in her paws again.

"Of a sort," Twiggy said.

"*The only sort.*" It was the snake's voice, hissing but not singing. Not distant. Not imagined.

From the corner of her eye, Witch-Hazel saw the snake's gold eyes and hypnotic swaying. She tried to turn her head away, but her eyes betrayed her, seeking out the sight she feared.

The snake rose out of the largest sarcophagus, a stone tomb with its heavy lid ajar. The sarcophagus was placed at the head of the room, blocking the path to the wide stairway up. Sinuous and mesmerizing, the snake slithered out of the sarcophagus and held its head high. Stretched upward, the snake was taller than any of them, even the lanky otter Fish-Breath. Witch-Hazel hadn't realized the size hidden in those coils when the snake had sung to her from under a bush so very long ago.

"You've brought me my treasures," it hissed, all the music gone from its voice. "No longer lost."

Twiggy and Fish-Breath turned to Witch-Hazel, questioning, confused.

"I have nothing," she said. "Not even the candle crystals. They've all been lost or burned out. The last one burned out yesterday. You gave me barely enough."

The snake swayed, a reed of grass bending in an illusory wind. A forked tongue flicked out of its coyly smiling, scaly face. "My magic has drawn you here, and you will give my treasure to me."

"I have nothing." Witch-Hazel made a show of taking off her knapsack and satchel. She upended the knapsack, deftly and subtly holding shut the small inner pocket that held the circlet and ring. Then she flung the satchel, entirely empty now, back at the snake who'd gifted it to her. "I almost lost myself on your fool's errand," Witch-Hazel challenged the snake. "Now I'm going home."

"Not until you turn over the Celestial Fragments," the snake hissed, forked tongue flickering like a black flame.

"Don't you understand?" Fish-Breath cried. "They're lost forever!" The otter balled his webbed paws into angry fists. "They were buried in an avalanche with the castle at the heart of the eternal river …" He turned away, hiding his tears. Twiggy put a comforting paw on his shoulder.

The snake's yellow eyes narrowed, and their golden glow took on a molten hue. Lava burned in those eyes, fierce, hot, and ready to burn the little squirrel to ash. "You lied to your friends as well as the raven. Oh, yes, I heard you lie to the librarian. And I saw you unleash Celestial light in the magnolia tree. And I watched you take my payments for your work—you ate the mushrooms, used the candle crystals, followed the lanterns I lit. You owe me. I've followed you, and you've done with your paws what I could not do with my coils and magic. And now you will turn over my treasures."

The snake's eyes glowed brighter and brighter, their redness changing the light in the room to a ruddy, bloody tone. But Witch-Hazel wasn't watching the snake's eyes—she was watching the pain and hurt in Fish-Breath's.

"You found the Celestial Fragments?" Fish-Breath asked.

Witch-Hazel nodded, mutely, struck dumb by her own betrayal of her friend.

"All three of them?" Twiggy pressed. "Enough to ascend to meet the All-Being?"

Witch-Hazel opened her mouth to answer. Before she could speak, Zwi flew past her ear and buzzed, "*We don't have time for this. Run.*"

The yellow-and-black speck zig-zagged away. Witch-Hazel grabbed the circlet and ring from their hidden pocket, discarded her knapsack on the floor, and scampered after the bee, straight toward the snake blocking their path.

When Zwi got to the snake, she spiraled, corkscrewing through the air around the long swaying body, buzzing louder than Witch-Hazel had ever heard her. Distracted by the frenetic buzzing, the snake's hypnotic sway faltered. The red glow in its eyes dimmed back to molten gold.

The snake snapped its spade-shaped head at the flitting insect, but Zwi flew too fast. She led the snake in a merry little jig of long-spined shimmies before zipping away toward the stairs. Witch-Hazel and the others were already pounding their way up the twisting flight.

17

THE SANCTUARY OF THE CHURCH echoed with the snake's song. Its musical hiss bounced eerily off the high ceilings and along the empty pews, a cruel trick, making it sound like the snake was all around them instead of still slithering up from behind.

Stained glass windows stretched up to the peaked stone ceiling, depicting the All-Being exactly as Witch-Hazel had imagined—facets of every creature combined into an epic chimera; the best of every creature; a rainbow of life. All the kaleidoscopic glass needed was sunlight to dance and sparkle. Instead, the colors lay fallow, muted. All the windows were backed with dirt. They were still underground.

Twiggy and Fish-Breath ran to the front doors, but they must have been backed with dirt as well. They wouldn't budge. Zwi flew high into the spired ceiling, buzzing up to the darkened glass and into the corners of the stone architecture, but there was no way out.

They were still underground.

Witch-Hazel stood in the center of the sanctuary. She wondered how deep underground they were. She had doubted Twiggy's measurements and Zwi's instincts. And all along, she had been following a trail left for her by the snake. This was the snake's church. It could be anywhere. It could be in the very heart of the earth, far past the castle, approaching the edge of hell itself.

The snake had drawn her here. Now she must face it. She had no firethorn swords. No sword of the mole cleric. No tarnished copper pot. She had already drunk the potion of strength from the leontaur.

All she had were the Celestial Fragments.

A small voice in the back of her mind screamed, *And friends! You have friends!* But she could see her friends, scrabbling at blocked doors and flying around, exploring the ceiling for escapes that didn't exist. They were useless.

The snake was powerful.

In spite of herself, Witch-Hazel hated her friends for their powerlessness. She'd failed them by leading them into the snake's trap, but it was easier to feel like they'd failed her. It would be easier to watch them die if she could blame them for their own deaths.

Witch-Hazel walked back toward the stairs on the right side of the church's sanctuary, leaving Twiggy and Fish-Breath to beat at the solid doors of the church's front entrance. Zwi continued buzzing in the air far above.

The snake slithered up the stone steps toward Witch-Hazel, followed by dozens of lizards and serpents, hissing and rotting, scales flaking off and chunks of flesh missing, raised from their sleep of death by the blood magic glowing in their leader's eyes. This is what had been hiding inside those stone sarcophagi. Dead lizards. Dead snakes. Zombies with dull eyes and reeking with the stink of death. Most of them were smaller than Witch-Hazel, but she didn't want to fight them. She shuddered at the idea of even touching their sickly dead flesh.

Witch-Hazel wanted to hand over the treasures to the snake, bargain for her own safety, beg to be led back to the sunlight. But this wasn't the snake she remembered singing to her from under a bush on a sunny day. This was a necromancer of darkness, leading an army of the undead. She couldn't bargain with it. She'd be gambling in a game where the prize was death, the risk undeath. She might as well place herself in the snake's poison-dripping mouth. It would be better to go down fighting.

Witch-Hazel looked frantically around the sanctuary of the buried church, hoping to spot potential weapons. Anything long and hard or sharp; anything she could tear off a wall or pull out of the ground … There was nothing. Wooden pews, too long and large and solid to lift, and a smooth stone floor under dark stained-glass windows. There weren't even statues; no ornate decorations that could be broken from the walls and repurposed.

Though, Witch-Hazel thought, she could do something with the glass from the darkened windows. If only she had a way to break them.

"Twiggy," Witch-Hazel called. "I need your frame pack."

The beaver turned from the wide wooden door she was wrestling with to stare transfixed at the slithering army of scaly zombies. Witch-Hazel rushed over to her, wrestled the frame pack off of the beaver who'd been shocked and scared into near immobility. Twiggy and Fish-Breath hadn't faced dark squirrels and ghost moles like Witch-Hazel had. They weren't prepared for the hideous, stomach-churning sight of the snake's army.

Witch-Hazel had been hardened and forged by her journey. She wouldn't let an army of rotting reptiles best her.

Witch-Hazel dumped out the remnants of supplies in the frame pack. Most of them were useless—spoons and small bowls. But there was one thing she could use: when the last candle crystal had burned out, Twiggy had asked to keep it. Witch-Hazel had no use for the lightless rock, and she'd been discarding them when they stopped glowing. But Twiggy insisted that she wanted to keep one to examine and study when she got home to Riverton.

A single globe of stone wasn't much of a weapon, but it could break a stained glass window. Witch-Hazel grabbed the stone firmly, readied her arm, and threw it as hard as she could toward the closest window—a pastoral depiction of a red-gold koi swimming through a purple-blue lake. The colorful glass shattered, falling to the floor in glinting shards and sparkling slivers, mixed with sprinkles of dirt. Witch-Hazel stepped lightly, keeping to the edge of the ring of broken glass and dirt, searching for the largest shard she could reach without stepping onto the dagger-sharp splinters.

She found a piece of glass—blood red and shaped like a jagged-edged teardrop—that had been one of the tail fins of the koi fish itself. She picked the shard up gingerly in her paws. She had no way to use it. There was no time to bind it to a handle. Even if she could rip a strip of cloth from her little blue coat and wrap the shard of glass tightly against one of Twiggy's spoons … It would be a horrible weapon.

She would have to fight with teeth and claws. They were all she had. She would surely die.

Witch-Hazel dropped the shard of glass, turned to face the advancing army, slithering and shambling toward her. She screamed at them: "I will tear you all to pieces; there won't be enough of you left to meet the All-Being."

"Big words from my Clever-Brave squirrel," the snake hissed from across the rows of pews. "I wonder if Clever-Brave squirrels taste better than stupid-weak ones. All the ones who failed. The stringy, gamy ones." The snake's forked tongue flickered, punctuating its words.

The snake meant Salal-Berry.

"How dare you—" Witch-Hazel sputtered. In her anger, she charged across the sanctuary, running between the pews until she could stare the snake in the eye unobstructed. The reptile swayed hypnotically, safely behind its army of smaller reptilian zombies.

"This squirrel's not alone!" Fish-Breath squeaked, his voice high-pitched with anger. "And I won't let you eat her!" The otter rushed at the army of rotting lizards, coming at their ranks from the side. He ripped into the first lizard he encountered, tearing its rotting arm off with his webbed paws. His arms were short, but he was four times the size of most of the lizards. The next one he picked up, Fish-Breath ripped in half at the middle. Once the otter dropped both halves back on the stone floor, the lizard's halves crawled toward each other, twitching and spasming; its eyes rolled back, and its head shook like it was suffering a seizure.

The angry otter mowed through lizards, shedding their broken bodies left and right, and then stomping on them as they twitched with his webbed hind-feet.

He was glorious, a true woodland hero in his green jerkin and glossy brown fur. The lizards and snakes were nothing. Already dead; they'd traded their peaceful repose in luxurious sarcophagi for lying broken and trod upon on the sanctuary floor. It did not look like a good trade.

Emboldened by Fish-Breath's attack, Witch-Hazel and Twiggy followed the otter's lead. Twiggy thwacked rotting reptiles with her broad tail and sent them soaring to slam against the stone walls of the sanctuary. Witch-Hazel clawed at the reptiles' faces, scratching out their eyes, and trying not to remember the sightless crab sorcerers. This was different. The crabs had been mad, but these reptiles were worse than mad—they were already dead. They had no need of eyes.

They also had no need of air. Witch-Hazel learned that the hard way when she tried to strangle one—with its windpipe crushed, the zombie lizard kept struggling, clawing at her with its scaly hands. She tried to rip its head off, but she wasn't as strong as Fish-Breath. Witch-Hazel settled for tearing off its jaw, kicking it in the stomach, and scrambling away.

The three mammals—and Zwi now, buzzing about, stinging the dead reptiles in their faces—were holding their own, but there was no way to win. New zombie reptiles kept slithering up from the catacombs, and even the dead ones pulled themselves back together, raised again and again by the demonic red glow emanating from the snake's eyes. Eventually, even the peaceful skeletons of mammals that had lain on shelves along the walls below the sarcophagus room began fulfilling Witch-Hazel's nightmarish fears and clattered their way up the stairs to join the battle. Their bony bodies jerked about like evil marionettes hung on invisible strings.

Witch-Hazel missed her firethorn swords. She couldn't fight off skeletons so easily without them—their long bones struck her back and shoulders with bruising blows and knocked her head, leaving her vision spinning. Witch-Hazel scurried away from the fray, jumping from the back of one pew to the next, until she was back at the shards of glass from the broken window. She grabbed the red teardrop shard again, determined this time to make a weapon of it. But in her hurry, she sliced a pawpad on the glass's jagged edge.

Red blood smeared across the blood-red glass. The glass, cold against her paw, felt wet; the stiff teardrop shape skewed, drooping, until it flapped in Witch-Hazel's paw like a fish fighting to breathe. The shape grew and stretched, too large to fit in Witch-Hazel's paw. It fell to the ground, flopping, gasping, larger than a squirrel. It truly was a koi fish gasping for air.

Witch-Hazel dug into the hidden pocket in her knapsack, pulled out the ring with the Moon Opal, and held the glimmering gem—the Celestial Fragment that could bestow Endless Breath—out to touch the fish.

As soon as the milky-bright opal touched the koi fish's O-shaped lips, the glass all around—broken fragments of the blue stained-glass pond the koi had been swimming in when it was only a picture in the window—melted together, forming an inexplicable pool in the otherwise flat stone floor. The koi fell in with a splash, flicked her tail, and swam in a small circle. She looked like living gold.

Witch-Hazel slipped the Moon Opal ring on one of her fingers, hoping its powers hadn't been used up. Or maybe it would be better if they were—then the Celestial Fragments would be worthless to the snake when it finally stole them.

After a few circles dimpling the surface of the blue pond, the koi fish poked her head back out of the water; her face was bewhiskered with tentacles; her eyes were round like coins. She flipped her red-finned tail, and the light danced on the unsettled surface of the deep blue pool. In the shifting light, Witch-Hazel noticed a circlet of filigree gold blending in with the red-gold scales on the back of the koi's head. Another queen. The fish's voice was mellifluous and sad when she spoke to the bewildered squirrel: "You've summoned me, Queen Kokeu of the water realm with blood and desperation, and I owe you a blessing. But I've been watching, and this is not a battle you can win without a steep cost."

"What cost?" Witch-Hazel asked.

"I cannot tell you the cost. All I can offer is a blessing."

"Okay, then, what blessing?"

"I can summon all the water-dwellers away from this battle," Queen Kokeu said. "Many of the undead lizards and snakes who are here should have passed into my realm long ago. They'll be happy in my water realm, at rest finally."

"All the water-dwellers?" Witch-Hazel asked, wary of a catch. She glanced over her shoulder to see Twiggy thwacking skeletons with her tail and Fish-Breath bopping them on their skulls with his webbed fists. "Except my friends, you mean? Except the beaver and the otter?"

"That is up to you. I can take the beaver and the otter along with the others or not. But know, your friends would be happy with me. And safe."

Witch-Hazel's ears flattened against her head as she considered the koi queen's words. *Happy* and *safe* when she said them sounded almost like a euphemism for death. "But then Zwi and I would be alone with the snake and whatever's left of the army …"

"Half of the army," the koi said. "And, yes. Choose fast."

"Then don't take them," Witch-Hazel blurted. Twiggy and Fish-Breath didn't belong in some alternate water dimension. They belonged here with her—they would escape somehow and return to Riverton. Together.

"Very well," the koi queen said, stretching her O-shaped mouth into an oblong smile. She splashed her tail and swam, faster and faster, in tiny circles, whipping the inexplicable pool into a whirlpool. Faster and faster. Upward and out. The whirlpool twisted up off the ground and into a cyclone—blue and purple and transparent like the stained glass it had come from. The cyclone tore through the room, sweeping up zombies and skeletons in its path. Half it left alone. Half shone through its glassy glaze, complete again inside its funnel: lizard zombies regained their scales and scintillated green and whole; otter skeletons regained their flesh and fur. It was magic and powerful and momentarily, it was gone.

Witch-Hazel surveyed the devastated army. The remaining skeletons were unfazed—squirrel and fox bones jerked about, still macabre marionettes intent on destruction. The remaining zombies, though, had halted in their fighting. Cloudy eyes blinked, and arms covered in dull patchy scales lowered to their sides. Rotting tongues muttered, "Why didn't I ascend?" and "Where is my second awakening?"

The necromancer snake hissed to its undead disciples, "That was not the second awakening, fools! Those idiots were swept away from their true awakening by a lesser deity than the one we seek—get the Celestial Fragments from that squirrel, and I'll show you the All-Being!" The snake pointed at Witch-Hazel with its green spear of a tail and its black forked tongue.

Witch-Hazel's fur prickled all down her neck as she realized the army of zombies and skeletons was no longer letting itself be distracted by the much larger mammals who'd been fighting them. Now they were all headed directly toward her, bones rattling and rotting limbs shambling.

Witch-Hazel leapt onto the back of a pew and from there jumped straight up the cathedral wall and sank her claws into the packed dirt behind the stained glass window she'd broken. Squirrels can jump high, and their claws dig deep. She clung to the vertical dirt and scrambled upward as if the dirt were tree bark.

When she reached the edge of the broken glass, Witch-Hazel looked down to see the army of zombies and skeletons gathered beneath her. Some of them had begun scaling the church's stone wall, following her upward as well.

"I can't climb the glass," Witch-Hazel called down to her friends. "Can you clear my way? Throw the candle crystal and break the glass."

Fish-Breath found the round stone where it had been discarded on the floor, and he threw it at the glass patterns above Witch-Hazel. Her ears flattened as glass rained down around her in colorful shards. Then she began climbing higher. The otter threw the candle crystal several more times, clearing a path of naked dirt all the way up to where the church wall angled into the ceiling.

Cowering in the corner between dirt wall and stone ceiling, Witch-Hazel was ready to give up. It was time to find the most painless way to die—ideally, a way in which the snake wouldn't raise her bones as an evil skeletal marionette. Then she noticed something that gave her hope: a tawny, twisty, tendril of root. Not the kind of thick woody root that one would find deep, deep beneath the earth. This was a flower root—soft and pliant. The surface was near. Witch-Hazel scratched at the dirt and found more tangles of the hanging blonde root. She scratched and clawed, breaking away the dirt in clumps and clods that fell down on the skeletons climbing toward her.

Suddenly, the dirt gave way beneath Witch-Hazel's claws, and she fell. She fell past climbing skeletons, her brushy tail twirling for balance in the air and her paws spread wide as if she could slow her fall by spreading herself into a tiny parachute. She expected the wind to be knocked out of her by glass-gritted stone any moment. But instead she landed in broad furry arms.

"Gotcha," Fish-Breath breathed. The otter's expression was serious and dour, but his long white whiskers sparkled with sunlight. Actual sunlight. Witch-Hazel looked up and saw the dirt she'd been scratching away had broken through—she saw blue sky above, and a single beam of golden sunlight streamed down, glowing in the dusty air. The golden light fell like a spotlight on her and Fish-Breath.

"Zwi!" Witch-Hazel cried, climbing from Fish-Breath's arms onto the back of a pew. She waved her paws wildly, trying to capture the bee's attention. "Come quickly! There's sunlight!"

The tiny bee hovered, still in the air for a moment, paused in her stinging torment of a rotting one-armed lizard. Then with a swooping, buzzing swoosh, Zwi swerved through the cathedral hall toward Witch-Hazel. She zipped between scaly zombies and flew straight through one large badger skeleton's rib cage.

Witch-Hazel pulled the Star Sliver on its silver chain from the hidden pocket in her knapsack and held it out in one paw. With the other paw, she lifted the golden sunflower pendant from her breast and yanked the chain over her head; it caught briefly in the notch she'd earned on her left ear.

The topaz-like Sun Shard gleamed so brightly in the beam of true sunlight that Witch-Hazel squinted her eyes and cringed. As her eyes adjusted, she saw rainbows of aurora borealis dancing in the air—a hundred times brighter and a thousand times more colorful than they'd been in the magnolia tree. Shades of butter yellow, lavender violet, and cornflower blue glinted off the smooth surface of the Moon Opal, still worn on Witch-Hazel's paw, and the dangling Star Sliver shone with a silvery light unlike any she had imagined before. It was full of twilight and mystery and wonder.

"Hurry, Zwi—" Witch-Hazel fumbled with the Moon Opal ring, until it slid over her pawpad. Clearly, its power wasn't spent, and she didn't want to waste that power on herself. She needed to stay here with Fish-Breath, but if

Zwi could ascend to meet the All-Being, there'd be nothing left for the snake to steal from her. Its evil plan would be foiled, and Witch-Hazel felt confident that then she could beat it. She'd already stolen away half the snake's army.

The bee landed on Witch-Hazel's outstretched paw, but before the squirrel could affix the ring to Zwi's head, a tiny coronet around her waving antennae, a shriek let out behind them. It was Fish-Breath's voice. And it was a mortal scream.

"No!" Twiggy and Witch-Hazel cried the word as one, before they'd even seen the damage.

The badger skeleton, fully as large as any otter, had sunk its sharp teeth into Fish-Breath's neck. Blood gushed into the otter's thick brown fur and soaked his green jerkin. He swooned, crashed, and leaned against the wooden pew, and then fell to the ground. He wouldn't last long.

The beaver rushed to her friend's side, flinging away any skeleton or zombie that crossed her path. Witch-Hazel knelt over the dying otter, and Zwi landed on his shoulder, beside the rushing blood. Her tiny forelegs waved frantically, as if she were looking for some way to stem the tide of red.

Twiggy hiccoughed with sobs and clutched Fish-Breath's paw.

Witch-Hazel said, "You can't go—I need you to take me to Riverton." Her heart was breaking. She could have sent Fish-Breath away, mere minutes ago, to live safely in a water realm ruled by a queen koi. Instead he was dying in her arms. She'd been so selfish. But there was still something she could do. One last hope.

"Don't stop breathing," Witch-Hazel whispered in his round ear as she slipped the Moon Opal ring onto the tip of Fish-Breath's webbed finger. His breath was coming out in gasps, but it smoothed once the ring was on.

"Be strong." Witch-Hazel placed the golden chain of the Sun Shard around Fish-Breath's bleeding neck and arranged the sunflower pendant carefully on his chest. Finally she fastened the silver circlet of the Star Sliver around his wrist. Witch-Hazel could barely get out the words between sobs: "Fly to the All-Being. Don't die."

Strength, flight, endless breath.

The power of the Celestial Shards had to save him.

The snake's angry hiss cut through the air. "Mine!" But then a new sound drowned it out—a song Witch-Hazel had heard before, but it wasn't sung by a serpent's slithery tongue this time. It was sung in harmony, so many voices, all together a choir singing the story of the All-Being.

It was a victory song. It was a lullaby.

Witch-Hazel looked around and saw the zombies and skeletons lying down. Their dead eyes closed. The red magic in the snake's eyes could no longer control them.

The church was filled with rainbows, tucking the poor lost souls into their eternal sleep. For good this time.

Twiggy yelped as Fish-Breath clasped her paw back. Strength had returned to him. The otter lifted his head, tilted it, testing the strength of his neck. Then he pushed his friends aside and rose up on his paws. Wings spread from his back—brown and feathery; otter wings, angel wings, wings to carry him to the All-Being. He flapped them and rose into the air as if drawn upward, his soul pulling him toward the sky.

The unbroken stained glass windows all around the cathedral shone as if they were backed by a million suns instead of by packed dirt. The colors broke free from their frames, danced and swirled, mixing with the rainbows that shone from Fish-Breath's Celestial jewels.

The eye that had looked down on Witch-Hazel before—as the avalanche had started—opened in the swirling vortex of colors and looked down on them all again. The singing chorus grew louder; it came from all around, drowning their ears with music as their eyes were dazzled by color and light.

Fish-Breath waved—a tiny, sad goodbye—as his wings carried him into the dark pupil of the All-Being's giant eye. The pupil narrowed as if the All-Being were staring into the sun, and the rainbow iris closed around the flying otter.

All that was left was rainbows and music.

And then not even those.

Darkness and silence. An empty church, littered with the remains of an army and a single seething snake.

Witch-Hazel grabbed the skeletal leg of the badger who'd bitten Fish-Breath. She tore off the longest bone and wielded the femur like a club. "Come a slither closer, and I'll bash your brain in," she threatened the snake.

The snake swayed like a pendulum, back and forth, considering the tiny squirrel who'd bested an army with the aid of a queen and the All-Being.

"You have nothing left that I want," the snake hissed before turning away. "Not even your death. Live a long life, Clever-Brave squirrel, missing your otter." The snake's forked tongue flicked, and then it turned away. It slithered back down the stairs to the catacombs in silence. No more singing. No more hissing.

No more snake.

Witch-Hazel dropped the femur and turned to Twiggy. "I can climb out of here, and Zwi can fly. What about you?"

"Don't worry about me." The beaver's voice was gruff. She shuffled to her frame pack, pulled apart the wooden frame, and improvised climbing stakes from two of the sharper spears of wood. She didn't climb gracefully, but with the stakes to stab into the dirt wall, she managed to hoist her round body upward a little at a time. Zwi flew ahead of her.

Witch-Hazel waited for Twiggy to climb all the way up the wall and squeeze through the hole in the dirt before following her.

The squirrel scurried quickly up and cried when her face broke through to the outside and she felt fresh air in her whiskers. Or maybe she'd already been crying.

Witch-Hazel tumbled onto the grassy earth and stared up at the blue sky. She halfway hoped to see Fish-Breath still flying up there in the ocean-deep blue, swooping and playing in the sky like he'd played in the rivulets underground—but his wings hadn't carried him up here. He'd flown somewhere else entirely. Somewhere with endless rivers. Somewhere he could feel the love of the All-Being, and maybe repair those rivers so they would flow between the layers of the world.

Somewhere he'd never know how much a damaged and scarred squirrel had loved him. How much she'd hoped to find happiness with him in Riverton.

Reminded of Riverton, Witch-Hazel pushed herself off the ground and looked for Twiggy. The beaver was already waddling away through the field of grass.

"Are you going home to Riverton?" Witch-Hazel called.

Twiggy didn't turn back.

Witch-Hazel darted across the field to catch up with her. "Can I come with you?" She didn't think she could return to her own home. Not right now. She couldn't tell her sisters and brothers where she'd been, all she'd seen and gained and lost, how badly she'd failed. Once again. She'd held treasure in her paws—a webbed paw, holding her own—and lost it all.

Twiggy turned around. Her eyes were red-rimmed and the fur under them matted with tears. Her shoulders slumped, and her tiny ears turned downward. "I can't …" she said. It sounded like there were more words to come, but they didn't come. Just a soft whistle between her teeth.

Witch-Hazel's own pointy ears sagged. They'd shared Fish-Breath's death and resurrection. The loss of that jolly otter. And that loss would always hang between them. If only Witch-Hazel hadn't hidden the fragments from her friends, maybe Fish-Breath would still be with them. "I understand," she said.

She watched the beaver trudge away.

Filled with prickly despair, Witch-Hazel needed the comfort of a tree's bark under her claws. She scurried across the field to the nearest tree—a silver maple with a broad trunk. She ran straight up its rough bark and then along a sturdy limb. With the silver bark under her claws, she stared out at the blue sky. A soft breeze moved the air, and a wispy cloud drifted over the sun. Witch-Hazel was alone. She might as well go home to her oak tree.

Then a speck in the distance zoomed her way, tiny, black-and-yellow, and buzzing as it came closer.

"I thought you'd gone," Witch-Hazel said to the bee.

"You gave my Celestial Fragments away," Zwi buzzed, hovering in the sunny air.

"I had to," Witch-Hazel answered.

"I know." Zwi flew several circles around the squirrel before landing on her shoulder. "He was a good otter."

Witch-Hazel's chest shook with a suppressed sob. "Do you think …"

"He'll ever return?" Zwi fluttered her tiny wings. "I don't know. The All-Being is mysterious."

Witch-Hazel cried, and Zwi let her. She pictured Fish-Breath returning to her someday in the rapids of a river flowing down from the sky, blue as the sky but wetter. Maybe then Twiggy would forgive her. They could all be together again.

Twiggy and Fish-Breath had no idea how much they had widened Witch-Hazel's world, how much hope and joy and confidence they'd given to her. She was a better squirrel for having known them.

When Witch-Hazel's sobs subsided, the bee said, "I still need to find a tree for my hive."

After several long moments, Witch-Hazel managed to say, "Squirrels are good with trees."

"I know that too." Zwi buzzed back into the air. "Come with me," she said. "My quest isn't finished, and it's better to quest together."

Witch-Hazel had nothing else. But this bee shared some of her memories of Fish-Breath, and carried a strange hope: the vision of a hive newly settled in a sanctified tree, blessed by the All-Being.

"Yes, I'll come."

The bee swerved off through the maple grove, coasting along invisible currents in the air, and Witch-Hazel followed, jumping from branch to branch, tree to tree, unsure where this quest might take her but unready to go home. One quest to the next, no longer guided by a song.

Maybe someday, Witch-Hazel would make her own song.

About the Author

Mary E. Lowd lives in Oregon with her husband, daughter, son, a bevy of cats and dogs, the occasional fish, and a neighborhood full of squirrels. She spends the majority of her time pretending animals can talk and writing stories about them. The animals, stories, and Mary reside in a crashed spaceship disguised as a house, hidden inside a fairy's garden.

More than one hundred of Mary's short stories have been published, and *The Snake's Song* is her fifth novel. Her previous novels include the *Otters In Space* trilogy and its spinoff *In a Dog's World.* Her fiction has won an Ursa Major Award and two Cóyotl Awards. She also edits the annual anthology series, *ROAR*, for FurPlanet.

www.marylowd.com

The Original

DUNGEON SOLITAIRE

Tomb of Four Kings

Still Available for Free
at
matthewlowes.com/games

Complete Rules
are Print-Ready and Playable
with any Standard Deck
of Playing Cards

Dungeon Solitaire
Labyrinth of Souls
TAROT CARD GAME
by Matthew Lowes
Illustrated by Josephe Vandel